In the Arms
of the Rancher

JOAN HOHL

D1333331

First published in Great Britain 2010
Large Print edition 2010
Harlequin Mills & Boon Limited,
Eton House, 18-24 Paradise Road,
Richmond, Surrey TW9 1SR

© Joan Hohl 2009

ISBN: 978 0 263 21582 3

Harlequin Mills & Boon policy is to use papers that
are natural, renewable and recyclable products and
made from wood grown in sustainable forests. The
logging and manufacturing process conform to the legal
environmental regulations of the country of origin.

Printed and bound in Great Britain
by CPI Antony Rowe, Chippenham, Wiltshire

JOAN HOHL

is a bestselling author of more
than sixty books. She has received
numerous awards for her work,
including a Romance Writers of
America Golden Medallion award. In
addition to contemporary romance,
this prolific author also writes
historical and time-travel romances.
Joan lives in eastern Pennsylvania
with her husband and family.

My new editor, Krista,
and her assistant, Shana.
Welcome to my imaginary world!

Prologue

He needed a break, and he was going to take one. Hawk McKenna stood in the sunlight slanting from the west onto the covered porch that ran the width of his ranch house, his hand absently resting on the head of the large dog next to him.

Though the sun's rays were warm, there was a nip in the early October breeze. It felt good to Hawk after the long, hot, hard but productive and profitable summer. Yet he knew that before too long, the mild autumn would be replaced by snowflakes swirling, driven by harsh, bitter cold winds.

When the deep snows came, Hawk knew the work on the ranch would be just as hard as it had been during the summer. No, he thought, smiling wryly as he gazed around him at the valley in which his ranch was nestled, the work in the deep snows of winter entailed numb fingers and toes and being chilled to the bone. All things considered, he'd rather sweat than freeze.

The idea of what was to come sent a shiver through him. He must be getting old, Hawk mused, stepping from the porch into the fading sunlight. But as he was only thirty-six, perhaps it wasn't so much his age as it was tiredness. Other than a run into Durango, the city closest to the ranch, for supplies, he hadn't been off the property in months.

Nor had he been in any female company in all that time, other than that of his foreman Jack's nineteen-year-old daughter and his wrangler Ted's wife.

Not exactly what Hawk had in mind for female company. Ted's wife, Carol, while very nice and pretty, was…well, Ted's wife. And Jack's daughter, Brenda, was even prettier but far too young, and she was becoming a pain in the ass.

A year or so ago, Brenda, who had hung around the ranch every summer since Jack had come to work for Hawk, had begun trailing behind Hawk. Her sidelong, supposedly sexy glances were beginning to grate on his nerves.

He wasn't interested. She was a kid, for

cripes' sake. Not wanting to hurt her feelings, Hawk had tried dropping subtle hints to that effect, to no avail. She had gone right on with the sly, intimate looks, at moments even deliberately making physical contact, while making the touches appear accidental.

Frustrated, not knowing what to do other than be brutally honest by telling her to act her age and knock off her flirting, Hawk had approached Jack about her behavior. Treading as carefully as if he were negotiating a mine field, Hawk had asked him what Brenda's plans were for the future.

"Oh, you know kids," Jack said, grimacing. "They want everything. They just can't decide what in particular."

Hawk sighed. Not much help there. "It's over a year since she graduated high school. I thought she was planning to go on to college?"

"She now says she isn't sure." Jack gave him a probing look. "Why? Has she been making a pest of herself hanging around here?"

Drawing a slow breath, Hawk hedged. "Well…she has been kinda getting underfoot."

Jack nodded his understanding. "Yeah, I noticed," he admitted with a sigh. "I've been meaning to say something to her about it, but you know girls… They get so dramatic and emotional."

"Yeah," Hawk agreed, although he really didn't know girls, as in kids. He knew women, knew as well how emotional they could be. He worked hard at avoiding the dramatic ones.

"I'll talk to her," Jack said, heaving a sigh before flashing a grin. "Maybe I can talk her into spending the winter with her mother, as she always did while she was still in school." He chuckled.

Hawk shook his head. Jack and his former wife had not divorced amicably. Although Brenda had spent only the summers with Jack while she had been in school, mere days after receiving her diploma, she'd taken off, telling her mother she wanted to be on her own, *free*.

Well, Hawk mused, if being on her own and free meant living with her father while bugging the hell out of him, she had succeeded too well. "You handle it any way you want," Hawk said, not bothering to add that Jack had better handle it, and her, sooner rather than later. "Maybe a father-daughter heart-to-heart will help."

"Will do." Jack started to turn away.

"Hold up a minute," Hawk said, stopping

Jack short. "I'm going to take off for a couple weeks for a little R and R. Can you hold down the fort, and Boyo?" Hawk ruffled the hair on the dog's head.

Jack gave him a look. "You know damn well I can."

Hawk grinned. "Yeah, I know. I just like riling you now and again."

"As if I didn't know," Jack drawled. "You tellin' me where you're going and when?"

"Sure. No secret. I'm going to Vegas as soon as I can make room reservations. I'll let you know where I'll be staying." He paused before going on. "When I get back, you and Ted can take some time off. While I'm gone, you can decide who goes first."

"Good deal." Jack grinned and went back to work.

Relieved, Hawk drew a deep breath of the

pine-scented mountain air. The dog looked up at him expectantly. "Not this time, Boyo," he said, ruffling the dog's thick hair. "You'll be staying with Jack."

If a dog could frown, Hawk thought, that was exactly what the big Irish wolfhound was doing. With a final hair ruffle, he turned to the porch steps.

A smile on his lips, Hawk walked into the house, picked up the phone and began punching in numbers.

One

Kate Muldoon was behind the hostess station, checking the reservation list, when the restaurant entrance door opened. A smile of greeting on her lips, she glanced up to see a man just inside the door and felt a strange skip beat in her chest.

The first word to jump into her mind was *cowboy*. Kate couldn't say why that particular descriptive word came to mind. There wasn't a pair of boots or a Stetson in sight. He was dressed the same as most patrons, casually in jeans that hugged his hips like a lover, a pale blue button down shirt tucked into the narrow denim waistband, the sleeves rolled up to mid-forearm.

His height was impressive. Kate judged him to be six feet five or six inches tall at least, maybe more. He was lean, muscular and rangy. He had a head full of thick, straight dark, almost black, hair with strands of deepest red glinting under the lights. It was long, caught at his nape and was tied with a narrow strip of leather.

He was striking—sharply defined features, a squared jaw and piercing dark eyes. His skin was tanned, near bronze. Part Native American, perhaps? Maybe.

But he wasn't what she would call handsome, not in the way Jeff was....

"May I help you?" Kate asked brightly, pushing away errant thoughts of her former lover.

"I don't have a reservation, but I'd like a table for one, if you have it." His voice was smooth, low, rather sexy and alluring.

Telling herself to grow up, Kate said, "Yes, of course. If you'll follow me." Scooping up a menu, she ushered him to a small table for two set in a corner between two curtained windows.

He arched a dark brow with visible amusement when she slid out a chair for him. "Thank you."

"You're welcome," she replied, handing him the menu. "Tom will be your server today." Feeling oddly breathless, she added, "Enjoy your dinner."

He smiled.

Kate felt the shivery effects of his smile all

the way back to her station. Ridiculous, she chided herself, dismissing thoughts of the tall man when she noticed a line of unexpected guests waiting for her.

Greeting and seating the hungry patrons who had suddenly shown up snared Kate's focus. After seating a party of four nearest the corner table, she heard the tall man quietly call to her.

"Miss?"

The shivery effects began all over again. Sighing through her professional smile, she stopped at his table. "Can I get you something?" she responded, noticing his half-empty beer glass. He smiled, this time with a suggestive hint. Kate felt the shiver turn into an unnerving shimmering heat.

"Is Vic in the kitchen this evening?"

His question threw her for a moment. She

didn't know what she had expected, but an inquiry about her boss wasn't it. "Yes, he is," she answered, instantly regaining her composure.

"Would you give him a message from me?"

"Yes, of course." What else could she say?

"Tell him Hawk would like to talk to him." He smiled again, revealing strong white teeth.

"Hawk…just Hawk?" she asked. Lord, the man had a killer smile.

"Just Hawk," he said with a soft laugh. "He'll know who you mean."

"Uh…right. I'll tell him," Kate said, turning away to head for the kitchen. It was a good thing Jeff had immunized her against men, she thought, pushing through the swing door to the kitchen. That kind of man would get under an unwary woman's skin in a hurry.

* * *

That was one appealing package of femininity, he mused, his gaze fixed on the subtle yet intriguing movement of her hips as she pushed through the door to the kitchen. Of average height, she was all woman from the riot of loose curls in her long dark hair to her slim ankles, and everywhere in between. And he had noticed she wasn't wearing a ring on the third finger of her left hand.

Of course, that didn't necessarily mean she wasn't married. Hawk knew of many men as well as women who didn't wear their bands of commitment. Cramped their style, he supposed. He was wondering if she might be one of those women when a familiar voice broke into his musing.

"Hawk, you old dog, when did you get into

town?" Vic Molino came to a stop next to Hawk, a big smile of welcome on his handsome face, his right hand outthrust.

Rising, Hawk grasped the hand and pulled the shorter man into a buddy embrace.

Stepping back, Hawk flicked a hand at the empty chair opposite his. "Got a minute to talk…or are you too busy in the kitchen?"

Vic grinned. "Always got a minute for you, Hawk. How the hell are you?" He arched his dark brows. "It's been a long while since your last visit."

"Yeah, I know." Hawk grinned back. "Been too busy making money. Now, before winter sets in, I aim to spend a little of it."

"I hear you." As he spoke, a server came to a stop at the table. Vic smiled at him. "I'll take care of this customer, Tom, but you'll still get the tip." He lowered his voice dramatically, as if to prevent Hawk from hearing him. "And he's a big tipper."

Tom smiled. "Thanks, Vic." He turned to leave but Vic stopped him before he could take a step.

"One thing, Tom. You can bring me a pot of coffee." He shot a glance at Hawk. "You want a fresh beer?"

Hawk shook his head. "No, thanks. I'm going to have wine with dinner, but I would like a cup of coffee."

"Coming right up, sir," Tom said, hurrying away.

Hawk glanced around the dining room. "Business looks brisk, as usual."

"It has been good," Vic said, a touch of gratitude in his voice, "even with the slump in the economy." He pulled a frown. "I didn't even get a vacation this year."

Hawk gave him a droll look. "Poor baby. Lisa cracking the whip over you, huh?"

Vic flashed a white grin. "Never. My bride is too much in love with me to find fault."

Hawk felt a touch of something—longing, an empty sensation. Surely not envy for his friend and the bride he'd married over five years ago.

"In fact," Vic went on smugly, "Lisa's too happy at the present to find fault with anyone." He paused, waiting for the look of confused curiosity to bring a frown to Hawk's face.

"Well," Hawk said. "Where's the punch line?"

Vic gave a burst of happy laughter. "She's pregnant, Hawk. After all this time, all the praying and hoping, we're going to have a baby."

Hawk lit up in a smile. "That's wonderful, Vic. When's the baby due?"

"In the spring. She's in the beginning of her second trimester."

"Damn! Damn, that's great, for both of you. I know how much you've wanted a child." Even as he congratulated his friend, Hawk again felt that twinge of empty longing. He brushed it off as he shook Vic's hand.

"Yeah," Vic said, grinning like a kid. "We were almost at the point of accepting that there would never be a baby for us."

Grinning back at him, Hawk raised his glass of beer. "Well, here's to perseverance." Bringing the glass to his lips, he downed the beer remaining in it. As he set the glass down, the hostess came to the table with a full fresh pot of coffee.

"Tom was busy at another table," she explained. "So I brought this over. Is there anything else, Vic?"

"No thanks." Vic shook his head. As she started to turn away, he stopped her by taking her hand. "Wait a minute. I want you to meet an old friend."

"Okay." She smiled at Hawk.

He felt an instant of breathlessness. He stood up as Vic rose from his chair.

"Hawk," Vic said, "this lovely lady is Kate Muldoon, my hostess and Lisa's and my friend." He smiled at her. "Kate, Hawk McKenna. We've been friends since college, and he's been Lisa's friend since our wedding." A teasing gleam shone from his eyes. "I suspect she'd have grabbed him if she'd met him earlier."

"Right," Hawk drawled, offering his long-fingered hand to her. "Nice to meet you…Kate?"

"Of course," she answered. "Hawk?"

"Of course," he echoed.

"Have a seat, Kate," Vic said, rising to grab an empty chair at the next table while beckoning to someone.

Kate shook her head. "I can't, Vic. There are custom—"

"Yes, you can," Vic interrupted. "You haven't had a break yet."

Kate gave him a dry look. "I started working only two hours ago."

"Long enough," Vic said, turning to the young woman who had come to a halt at the table.

"You employed the imperial wave, sire?" the woman said, her blue eyes fairly dancing with amusement.

Vic laughed as he watched her give a quick glance at Hawk, her eyes widening with surprise. "Hawk!"

"Hi, Bella." Hawk said, getting to his feet just in time to catch her as she flung herself into his arms. "Subdued as ever, I see." Taking her by the shoulders, he set her back a step to look at her. "And beautiful as ever."

"I bet you say that to all your friends' sisters," Bella said, laughing. "You look great, Hawk."

"Thanks." Hawk smiled. "So do you."

"If this ritual of mutual admiration is over," Vic said, "I'd like you to take over at the desk for Kate for a while."

"Sure." Bella gave Hawk another quick hug before turning away. "Will I be seeing you while you're in town, Hawk?"

"Of course." Hawk smiled.

"Good." Bella smiled back. "Take your time, Kate. I can handle the ravenous crowd."

"Thanks, Bella," Kate said. "I'll only be a few minutes."

Her soft, almost smoky-sounding voice, along with her smile, caused an even stronger searing sensation in Hawk's stomach and sections south.

"So," Vic said, "how long are you going to be in town this time, Hawk?"

"I haven't decided yet. I have a room for a week." Hawk shrugged. "After that… depends."

"On what?" Vic laughed. "The weather?"

Hawk grinned. "Yeah, the weather. You know how much it concerns me." He shook his head. "No, actually, if I'm tired of the whole scene at the end of a week, I'll head home. If not, I'll make other arrangements."

"And where is home, Hawk?" Kate asked.

"Colorado," Hawk said. "In the mountains."

She laughed. "Colorado is full of mountains."

A tingle skipped the length of his spine. He drew a deep breath, willing steel to chase the tingle from his back. "I'm in the southwest corner, in the San Juans, a double jump from Durango."

"A double jump?" she said.

Vic answered for him. "Hawk's got a horse ranch in a small valley in the foothills there," he said. "I gotta tell you, this guy breeds and trains some gorgeous horseflesh."

"And I'm damned good at it, too," Hawk drawled around a quick smile.

Once again he felt that strange reaction to the conversation, a reaction he had never felt before. Hawk wasn't sure he liked it.

They chatted for a few moments longer. Then Kate excused herself to get back to work.

Unaware of his surroundings, Vic, or the soft sigh he expelled, Hawk watched Kate walk back to the hostess station, head high, her back straight, as regal as any queen.

"Attractive, isn't she?"

Vic's quiet voice jolted Hawk into awareness. "Yes," he said, shifting his gaze to his friend.

"And you're interested." It was not a question.

"Yes," Hawk admitted without hesitation.

"A lot of men are." Vic shrugged.

"I did notice she was not wearing a ring on her left ring finger." Hawk lifted his brows. "Is she attached?"

Vic shook his head. "No."

"Why do I have the feeling that if I said I wanted to ask her to have dinner one evening with me, you'd tell me she'll refuse?"

"Because she very likely would." Vic gave him a half smile. "She always does."

"She doesn't like men?" Hawk felt a sharp pang of disappointment.

"She used to," Vic answered cryptically.

Hawk's eyes narrowed. "Are you going to explain that murky statement, or am I going to have to call you out?"

Vic grinned. "Pistols at dawn, eh?"

"No…" Hawk drawled. "My foot in your rear right here in front of all your customers. So you'd better start explaining."

"There was a man…" Vic began.

"Isn't there always?" Hawk said in disgust.

"The same as there's always a woman with bitter men," Vic said. "Isn't there?"

"I wouldn't know." It was not a boast. Hawk had never been in love. He had no experience of how a relationship gone sour could rip a person up.

"You're a lucky man." Vic sighed. "Well,

Kate knows in spades. She was head over heels with a guy, enough to let him move in with her after they got engaged."

"He dumped her for another woman?" Hawk asked at the thought of any sane man dumping Kate.

"No, worse than that. Not long after he moved in with her, he became abusive."

Hawk stiffened, his features like chiseled rock. "He what?" His voice was low, icy with menace.

"Not physically," Vic said. "Verbally, which is just as bad, if not worse. Bruises heal pretty quickly. Emotional scars take a lot longer."

"The son of a bitch."

"That's my take on him."

Hawk was quiet a moment. "I'm still thinking of asking her to dinner one night." He frowned at Vic. "What do you think?"

"Well…" Now Vic was quiet a moment. He shrugged. "It can't hurt to give it a try."

"You wouldn't mind?"

"Why would I mind?" Vice shook his head. "I think it would do Kate good to get out… She hasn't been since she tossed the creep out." He grinned at Hawk. "And I know you'd never do anything to hurt her."

"How do you know that?"

Vic's grin grew sinister. "Because if you did, I'd have to kill you."

Hawk roared with laughter. "Get outta here and get me something to eat…and make it good."

Standing, Vic leveled a stern look at Hawk. "You know damn well everything I cook is good. Excellent, even."

"I know," Hawk admitted. "So, go cook."

Moments later he was served a glass of red

wine. Soon after the wine, the server set a steaming plate of pasta before him, with a short, folded note on the side. Hawk opened the note and chuckled. Vic had written just seven words.

Kate's days off are Monday and Tuesday.

Two

Kate didn't have time to think of anything except greeting and seating customers for over an hour. When she again returned to her station, she was both disconcertingly disappointed and pleased.

She needed a breathing break. What Kate didn't need were the thoughts of the attractive Hawk McKenna, which immediately flooded her mind.

He was just another man, she told herself. And yet he invaded her mind and senses the minute activity around her slowed. Shaking her head, as if she could physically shake the thoughts aside, she busied herself by fussing with the station. She straightened the large menus and made a production out of studying the names not crossed off on the long list of reservations. The few parties left on the list were not due to arrive for a while.

Sighing, she glanced up from the list, right into the dark eyes of the very man she had been trying her best not to think about.

She managed a professional smile. "How was your dinner, Mr. McKenna?"

He gave her a slight frown. "I thought we had agreed on Hawk and Kate."

"Okay. How was your dinner, Hawk?"

"Superb, as Vic's dinners usually are."

Kate felt the effects of his breathtaking smile all the way down to her curling toes.

"That's true," she managed to articulate around the sudden tightness in her throat. "Vic is a very talented chef. One of the best."

"I know." He nodded, a shadow of his smile lingering at the corners of his too-attractive mouth. "He was taught by another very talented chef…" He paused for effect. "His mother."

Kate laughed. It felt good to laugh with him. Too good. She quickly sobered. "I know," she said, sneaking a glance around him in hopes of finding a waiting patron. The entryway was empty.

"You expecting someone special?" he asked, obviously not missing her swift look behind him.

"No." She shook her head. "Why?"

Hawk studied her a moment. Kate felt strangely trapped, as if pinned to a board like a butterfly or some other species of insects.

"You're afraid of me, aren't you?" He was frowning again, this time in consternation.

"Afraid? Me?" She gave a quick and hard shake of her head. "That's ridiculous." She raked a slow look down the length of him, the long length of him. "Should I have a reason to fear you?" Kate was babbling, and she knew it. She just didn't know how to stop. "Do you mean me harm?"

"You're right. That is ridiculous, Kate." There was a note, a bit angry, a bit sad, in his soft voice. "I mean no harm to any woman. Why would you even think that?"

Kate bit her lip and closed her eyes. "I...I don't know...I..."

"Yes, you do." He cut her off. He drew a deep breath.

"That bastard really did a number on you, didn't he?" His voice was low, as if to make sure no one could overhear him.

Kate froze, inside and out. How did he know? Who told him? Vic, it had to have been Vic. The mere thought of Jeff, his nasty temper and his accusations caused a cold sensation in her stomach. Dammit, she thought. She had believed she was over it, free of the memories.

"Kate?" Hawk murmured, his soft tone threaded with concern.

Steeling herself, Kate looked him square in the eyes. "My personal life is not open for discussion, Mr. McKenna. I'd like you to leave, please. I have a party of four due any minute."

As if on cue the party swept into the lobby,

laughing and chattering. His face unreadable, Hawk stepped to one side, standing firm.

Kate conjured a pleasant smile and turned to face the new arrivals. "Good evening." Lifting four menus from the neat pile, she added, "Right this way."

After the patrons were seated and perusing their menus, Kate started back to the hostess station. Spotting Hawk—how could she miss him?—leaning against the side wall, she couldn't help noticing again how tall and lean and…

Don't go there, Kate, she advised herself, trying and failing to ignore the tiny twist of excitement curling around her insides.

She began feeling edgy as she approached the station. There wasn't a single person waiting in the foyer. She lifted her chin, prepared to glare at him for still being there.

Hawk didn't move but remained standing there, leaning one shoulder against the wall, his gaze fixed on her, a small, enticing smile curving his masculine lips.

His smile set off a new sensation in her body, one so intense she reached for anger in defense.

"You still here?" she said, inwardly cringing at having stated the obvious.

Hawk glanced down, then at the wall he was lounging against, then at her. "I do believe so. At least, it looks like me." His smile broadened, his eyes grew bright with a teasing light.

Kate suppressed a shiver of awareness as he pushed away from the wall and strolled to stand directly in front of her.

"Will you have dinner with me Monday or Tuesday evening?" he asked softly.

Nonplussed, Kate stared up at him. Surprise kept her silent. Raking her mind for a reply, she decided that she simply couldn't brush him off. He was a good friend of Vic's, besides being a customer. Still…the nerve of the man. She scowled at him while fighting a sudden urge to agree.

Foolish woman. She didn't even know him, trust him. She was afraid to trust any man, other than her father and Vic. Yet she was tempted to say yes to him.

"How did you know I was off Monday and Tuesday?" she said in a sad attempt at irritation.

He cocked his head.

She couldn't blame him, when the answer was so evident. Damn him. "Vic," she answered for him.

"Yes." Hawk nodded. "I can be trusted,

Kate," he said, voice soft, tone sincere. "And Vic will vouch for me. I promise not to step out of line."

Dilemma. What to do? Kate knew what she wanted to do. It had been so long, months since she'd been to dinner with a man.

Looking up at him, she stared into his dark eyes, seeing admiration and concern…for her.

Hawk leaned closer, against the station, his voice a bare, husky whisper. "Word of honor, I'll be good."

Kate relented. "Okay, Hawk, I'll have dinner with you Monday evening."

"That has got to be the hardest I have ever worked to get a date. What time and where can I pick you up?"

There was no way Kate was giving him her home address. "You can meet me here. Is seven-thirty okay?"

"Fine. I'll see you then." He raised a hand as if to respectfully touch his hat, which wasn't there. Grinning at her, he lowered his hand, gave a quick wave, turned and strode from the restaurant.

Bemused by his attractive smile, salute and even more so his laughter, Kate stared after him, kind of scared, kind of excited. Had she done the right thing in accepting his invitation, or should she have refused? Should she stay firmly hidden behind her barrier of mistrust for men?

Fortunately, Kate was temporarily relieved of the weight of the conundrum by the door opening to a family group exactly on time for their reservation.

By eleven forty-five, Kate, along with the other employees and the boss, had finished getting the place cleaned, the tables set and everything ready for the next day, Saturday, one of their busiest days.

As he did every night while the other male employees escorted the waitresses out, Vic walked Kate to her car, which was parked in the employees section of the parking lot. Kate used those few minutes to question Vic.

"Why did you tell your friend Hawk my days off?" She kept her voice free of inflection.

Vic slanted a wary look at her. "He asked. Are you angry at me for telling him?"

"No." Kate shook her head as she came to a stop next to her car.

"Just annoyed with me," he said. "Right?"

Kate met his direct gaze and smiled. "A bit, yes," she admitted. "You know how I feel about…" She paused, giving him a chance to speak over her.

"Yes, Kate, I know how you feel about men

in general and what's-his-name in particular. And I respect that." He shrugged. "But Hawk isn't any man in general, and not just because he's my friend. Hawk's one of the good guys, honey." He grinned. "You know, the ones who wear white hats in the cowboy movies." His grin widened. "Besides, I warned him that if you happened to accept his invitation, and he got out of line, I'd have to kill him."

Kate had to smile. "Well, I…um…I did agree to have dinner with him Monday evening."

"Good. It's time for you to get out and about again. Flirt a little. Hawk will love it, after being stuck in the mountains all summer."

"I'm sure I'll enjoy his company, Vic." Kate said. "But I don't believe I'm ready to flirt yet, if ever again."

"Well, if not this time, then sometime. Just

relax and enjoy a little." He glanced at his watch. "Now, I'd better be getting home to Lisa…before she starts getting suspicious."

"As if." Kate laughed. "Thanks, Vic. I'll see you tomorrow."

He waited until she had slid into the car, locked the doors and started the engine. With a quick wave, Vic headed for his own car.

Kate sat for a minute before pulling out of the lot. Although Vic's recommendation helped, she still felt a little nervous about the date with Hawk.

Drawing a deep, determined breath, she released the hand brake and drove away.

Two more days until Monday.

Excitement and trepidation pushed at her mind. Fortunately for Kate, Saturday evenings and Sunday brunches were always the busiest times in the restaurant. She barely had time to take deep breaths between greeting and seating patrons, never mind long enough to let herself indulge the nervous twinges playing havoc with her stomach.

Kate was relieved when it was finally time for her break Sunday evening.

She felt her entire body tighten with nerves when Vic joined her in the small employees' break room next to the noisy kitchen.

"Instead of enjoying a quiet break," he said, eyeing her critically, "you look as if you just heard terrifying news." His tone was only half kidding. "Would you like me to get in touch with Hawk and tell him you've changed your mind?"

Yes. The word immediately slammed into her mind. But Kate gritted her teeth, damned if she would chicken out.

She gave her head a quick shake. "No. I'll confess I'm a little nervous." She tried on a smile; it didn't fit. "But I have no intention of backing out of the date. I'm going to go and I'll enjoy the evening, as well." What a liar, she chided herself.

Vic's slip tightened as if to suppress a smile. She could tell he knew exactly how ambiguous she felt about spending the evening with Hawk…or with any other man, come to that.

Fortunately, Vic changed the subject and Kate managed to maintain her composure until quitting time.

Monday, 7:25 p.m.
Kate stood next to the hostess station, chatting with Bella. She was early. She had arrived at the restaurant soon after seven. She

was also nervous. She felt foolish about her anxiety, but there it was, like it or not.

Bella was seating customers. Kate was casting quick glances at the doorway, chiding herself every time she did, which by now was too often.

Kate glanced up as Bella returned to the station, just in time to see the young woman's face light up with a bright smile.

"Hi, Hawk," Bella said, quickening her step to launch herself into his open arms.

For an instant, a heartbeat, Kate felt the strangest emotion. She couldn't describe it exactly, but then, she didn't want to examine it, either, refusing to even think the word *envy*.

She allowed another word into her mind. *Breathtaking*. Hawk looked absolutely breathtaking. This evening he was dressed casually elegant in dark gray slacks, a crisp white shirt, no tie and a navy blazer.

Kate was relieved that she had taken extra time with her own attire. She had chosen a frilly-collared, long-sleeved sage blouse, a long, swirly nutmeg skirt and three-inch heels. While the days were still warm and even sometimes hot in October, the evenings dropped into the fifties and even the forties, so she had brought the same smooth fleece shawl that she had worn at work the previous night.

Bella swung out of Hawk's arms as a party of two entered. Hawk switched his dark gaze to Kate.

"Hi." His voice was soft, enticing.

Kate had to swallow before she could manage a rusty-sounding response. "Hi."

He slid a long glance the length of her body. "You look lovely."

She swallowed again. "Thank you. "Y-you look lovely, too." Good grief, Kate thought, feeling foolish. Had she really said that?

Hawk strolled to the hostess station, a smile flickering on his temptingly masculine lips. "Hungry?"

Watching his lips move, Kate felt as if the bottom had fallen out of her stomach. And in that moment she was hungrier than she'd ever been in her adult life. Yet the last thing on her rattled mind was food.

"Yes." She tried to unobtrusively wet her parched lips. "Are you?"

His eyes narrowing, he watched the slow movement of the tip of her tongue. "You have no idea," he murmured, reaching out a hand to take hers.

"W-where are we going?" Kate felt a flash of annoyance, not at Hawk, but at herself for the brief stutter again. Damn, she didn't stutter. Never had, not even briefly.

Hawk grinned. "Right here. Vic's creating something special for us."

"Here? We're staying here for dinner?" Kate had to laugh. "Why?"

His brows drew together in a dark frown. "You don't like Vic's cooking?"

"I love Vic's cooking," she protested. "It's just, well, I thought you would want to…"

"What I want, Kate," he declared, "is for you to feel comfortable with me, and I figured you would here." He smiled, then added, "With Vic to defend you."

"Right," Vic drawled, leading them to the same corner table for two that Hawk had been given a few days before. "As if I could defend her against you. I'm a chef, not a warrior."

"Cute. You're the one who works with

knives." Hawk shot Vic a wry look as he held a chair for Kate. "Wine?" he asked, folding his long body onto the chair opposite her.

Pondering their odd exchange, Kate nodded. "Yes, thank you." She glanced at Vic. "What do you recommend with the meal? White or red?"

"White for you," Vic said. "I think nothing too dry, nothing too sweet. You're both at my mercy with the meal tonight."

Hawk smiled dryly. "Right. I'll have the red. Room temperature.

"You know each other very well, don't you?" Kate said as Vic retreated to his kitchen.

"Hmm." Hawk nodded, taking a sip of his water. "We roomed together at college."

"Did you serve in the military?" Her question, seemingly coming out of nowhere, brought his eyebrows together in a brief frown.

"Yeah, after college I served in the air force. What made you ask that?"

Kate shrugged. "Vic called you a warrior, so I assumed that's what he was referring to."

His brows smoothed as he gave a soft chuckle. "I flew a Black Hawk chopper, but that wasn't what Vic was referring to," he said. "The warrior reference was to my heritage. You see, my father is Scottish, but my mother was a full-blooded Apache Indian."

"Was?"

"Yes, my mother died giving birth to my younger sister, Catriona." His smile was bittersweet. "I was two and never got to know her. All I have of her are pictures of her lovely face."

"I'm sorry," Kate said, at a loss for any other words of sympathy.

The bitter tinge vanished, leaving only the sweet. "Kate, it was a long time ago. I'm thirty-six years old. Though I'd have loved to have gotten to know her, I'm over it."

Somehow Kate doubted his assurance, but she didn't push. "Catriona. That's different," she said, changing the subject.

"It's Scottish for Catherine."

"What about your father?"

"He, with help from my mother's parents, raised me and Cat. After college I joined the air force. And after Cat graduated two years later, she moved to New York, and then Dad moved back to Scotland, where he owns several business holdings." A server appeared and Hawk took his glass. "He and his second wife raise Irish wolfhounds."

"Oh," Kate said. "They're really big and kind of mean, aren't they?"

Hawk's head was shaking before she finished. "They are big, but certainly not mean. I have one. His name's Boyo, and he's a pussycat." He hesitated before clarifying. "Of course, he can get ferocious if I'm in any way threatened. The breed is very protective of his people."

Kate had to laugh. "His people?"

"Oh, yeah." He laughed with her. "Boyo believes I belong to him."

They grew quiet when their meal was served, enjoying the sumptuous dinner Vic had prepared for them.

"Dessert? Coffee?" Hawk asked when they had both finished eating.

Kate shook her head. "No thank you. I'm too full for even coffee."

"Good." Hawk drew a quick breath. "It's nice here, but…" He took another breath. "I have tickets for a show on the strip. Would you like to go?"

Kate was quiet a moment, stilled by a little flicker inside, a combination of anxiety and expectation. As she had before, she drew a quick breath and made a quick decision. "Yes, thank you. I would."

Hawk shot a look at his watch, pushed back his chair and circled around the table to slide Kate's chair back for her to rise.

"We'd better leave. It's after nine and the show starts at ten." Hawk waved for their server. He said, "Check, please," when the server hurried over.

"No check," the server said. "Vic said this meal is on the house."

"Tom, you tell Vic I said he's a sweetie," Kate

said, smiling as the young man's cheeks flushed.

After quick goodbyes to Bella, they exited the restaurant.

Three

Taking Kate's elbow, Hawk steered her to the first parking space in the parking lot. Noting the makeshift Reserved sign tied to the light pole in one corner of the lot, Kate raised an eyebrow and looked up at him.

Hawk grinned at her. "It's good to be the king," he declared quoting from an old Mel Brooks movie.

The car he guided her to was midsize. After

she was seated, Kate watched, a slight smile
on her lips, as he crammed his long body into
the seat behind the wheel. Settled in, he
slanted a look at her.

"This king needs a bigger carriage."

"You do appear a bit cramped in that seat."

He rolled his eyes dramatically. "You have
no idea." He heaved a put-upon sigh. "At
home I drive a big-boy truck, with a large seat
and lots of legroom."

"This car is easier to fit into a parking
space," she said.

"Granted, but…" He smiled at her, smugly,
as he started the engine. "I don't have to park
it. I'm going valet." He paused an instant
before adding in a gotcha tone, "So there."

Kate lost it. Her laughter poured out of her
with genuine amusement. She couldn't recall
the last time she had laughed so hard, with

such ease. It was even better that Hawk was laughing right along with her.

As promised, he drove them to the valet parking at one of the casino hotels. The show, by a comedian Kate had never heard of before, was in one of the smaller entertainment rooms. The room was already full when they were escorted to their table just ahead of the burst of applause as the comedian strolled onto the stage.

The man wasn't merely funny; he was hilarious…and he worked clean. He didn't tell jokes. He told life, everyday things that just about every person in the room could relate to and appreciate.

The few times Kate shifted a quick glance at Hawk during the show, she found him laughing, too. One time he winked at her.

A simple wink, and yet it made Kate feel

warm all over. Silly woman, she chided herself.

Now, the show over, Kate moved to get up. Hawk stopped her with a shake of his head. "Want to go into the casino, play awhile before we leave?" he asked.

Kate hesitated. Then, remembering this was one of Jeff's favorite gambling sites, she shook her head. "Not tonight. I hurt from laughing," she said, smiling at him to soften her refusal. "He was very funny."

"Yes, he was," Hawk agreed, leading her outside. He handed over his parking ticket to the valet before adding, "And you're a lousy liar."

Kate opened her mouth, but before she could utter a protest, he said, "No insult intended."

"What would you call that remark?" Kate didn't attempt to conceal her annoyance.

The valet area was crowded with people

waiting for their vehicles. Hawk moved closer to her. "Kate," he said, his voice low, private, "I'm not unconscious. I saw the flicker in your eyes when you uttered that lame excuse. For some reason of your own, you don't want to go near that casino." He raised one dark brow. "Care to tell me why?"

He stood there, so close to Kate that she could smell his cologne and the pure masculine scent of him, and the tang of wine on his breath, teasing her lips. It played havoc with her nervous system.

"No?" He smiled.

She smiled, surrendering to his smile. "It's a silly thing, I guess," she said, sighing. "I didn't want to go in there, because that is one of Jeff's favorites." She shrugged. "I prefer not to run into him."

The instant she finished speaking, as if she had conjured him up, Jeff's practiced, cultured voice sent shivers of revulsion through her.

"Well, Kate. Beautiful as ever," he said, his voice and smile much too smooth. "Imagine seeing you here. I thought you didn't like the casinos." He acted as though Hawk wasn't there.

"You thought a lot of things, Jeff," she returned, her voice as cool as she could make it. "Most of them wrong...no, all of them wrong."

Jeff's pale blue eyes went cold; his smooth voice grew a jagged edge. "Not all of them." A leer twisted his lips as he ran a quick look over her. "I wasn't wrong about your response in the bed...."

"If you'll excuse me," Hawk interjected in

a menacing drawl, sliding one arm around Kate's waist. "The car's here, Kate."

Relief washed through her, but only for a moment. Jeff caught her by the arm, keeping her from moving away with Hawk. She stiffened, angry and embarrassed.

Jeff glared up at Hawk. And *up* was the word, as Hawk had a good six inches on the man. "Who the hell do you think you are?" he demanded.

"I don't think who I am," Hawk said. "I know who I am. And I don't want to know you." His drawl vanished, a soft warning taking its place. "Now, little man, take your hand off my lady."

"Little man! Your…your lady…" Jeff sputtered in anger. "You dare—"

Hawk sighed. "I. Dare. Anything." He enunciated very softly. "Now, back it up, buster, before I'm tempted to get real nasty."

To Kate's near amazement, Jeff took a step back, looking not at all like a cock of the walk, which was how he regularly portrayed himself. She watched him stare narrow-eyed at them as Hawk helped her into the car. But he blinked and took another step back as Hawk turned to stare back at him.

Although Kate couldn't see Hawk's face, she thought his expression must have looked meaner than hell, for turning on his heel, Jeff quickly strode back into the casino.

Turning her head, Kate watched, expecting to see a man ready to explode with anger, as Hawk came around the car and slid behind the wheel. To her utter surprise, she saw the brightness of inner laughter in his eyes and a grin on his rugged face. Amusement danced in his voice.

"I bluff at poker, too."

It started as a chuckle from Kate and developed into full laughter. "You're something else," she said, her laughter subsiding.

"Oh, lady, you don't know the half of it." Hawk slid his glance from the wheel after starting the car to toss a smile at her.

The tension of the previous minutes drained from Kate's body, leaving her relaxed and comfortable. For the first time since throwing Jeff, cursing and arguing, out of her apartment, and her life, she felt at ease in the company of a man.

Kate couldn't quite decide if that was good or not. She knew too well that being at ease with a man was not the same as trusting one. At this point in time, she wasn't sure she would ever again be able to trust a man, any man. It was sad, really, that one nasty male… She gave a mental shake. Forget him, she thought. He wasn't worth the effort it cost her to dwell on him. Resting her head back, she allowed her thoughts to drift.

They drove for several minutes, Kate content and mellow, before Hawk broke the mood.

"Er…Kate, are we going to drive around aimlessly for the rest of the night, or are you going to tell me where you live?"

Kate knew the mood was too good to last. "I parked my car at Vic's," she said, straightening from her near lounging position.

"Um," he murmured, making a turn at the next intersection. "We're a little past his restaurant."

Kate gave him a startled look before glancing around at the area. She frowned when she didn't recognize where they were. "How little?"

A smile twitched the corners of his mouth. "Oh, only a couple miles or so," he said. "You looked so comfortable, I hated to mention it. Fact is, I wasn't certain you were awake."

She felt her cheeks grow warm and was glad for the dark interior of the car. "I wasn't sleeping but I was drifting a bit. It must be the wine."

"All two glasses of it," Hawk drawled. Then he sobered. "Were you thinking about that clown who was giving you a hard time?"

"His name is Jeff," she said, tossing off the name as if it didn't matter, and it truly didn't.

"He grabbed your arm." His voice had changed. It was now close to a growl, almost scary. "And if he tries something like that again, touches you again when you're with me, his name will be sh—er—mud."

She had to chuckle at his quick word switch. "I do know the word, Hawk."

"I know. Everybody does." He shrugged.

"My father is a stickler for speaking politely in front of or to a lady. I feel the same way he does."

"That's nice." Kate said as he drove into the restaurant parking lot. He came to a stop next to her car in the otherwise empty lot.

Unfastening the seat belt, she turned to face him, offering her hand for him to shake. "Thank you, Hawk, for a lovely evening."

Although he took her hand, he shook his head. "I'm following you home, Kate."

"But…"

That was as far as he allowed her to get. "It's late, so I'll follow you and make sure you're safely inside." His voice was firm; he would brook no argument.

Shaking her head, she sighed and didn't argue. She got out of his car and into her own. True to his word, Hawk stayed on her tail, nearly tapping her bumper, until she pulled into the parking area of her apartment complex.

Once again he parked next to her. He got out of his car as Kate stepped from hers.

"I'll see you to the door," he told her.

"Really, Hawk, it's not necessary," she protested. She might as well have saved her breath. Without replying, he strolled beside her to the entranceway.

"Thanks again, Hawk," she said once more offering her hand to him.

"You're welcome." He took her hand and used it to gently draw her close to him. "Will I see you again?"

"Yes," was all Kate was capable of saying due to her suddenly dry throat.

"Tomorrow evening?"

She swallowed, hesitated before repeating, "Yes."

"Good." A mixture of relief and satisfaction colored his voice. "I'll pick you up here at seven-thirty, okay? We'll do something fun."

She nodded, her heart skipping when he raised his hand to cradle her face, his thumb slowly stroking her cheek. "That creep was right about one thing, Kate," he murmured, gently lifting her chin with the heel of his hand. "You are one very beautiful woman."

Now Kate's heart wasn't skipping; it was thundering.

"Hawk…I…"

"Shh," he murmured, lowering his head to hers. "It's all right. I won't hurt you." His breath whispered over her lips an instant before his mouth brushed over her mouth in what was not a kiss, but more a promise. "Good night, Kate." He stepped back. "Now, go inside and lock up."

Barely breathing and not thinking at all,

Kate went inside, unlocked the lobby door and ran up the stairs to her second-floor apartment, completely forgetting the elevator.

As Hawk slid behind the wheel of the rental, he glanced up at the building just as lights went on in the second-floor front apartment.

Staring at the glow through the sheer curtains on the windows, Hawk propped his elbows on the steering wheel.

Kate.

Surprisingly, as his lips had barely touched her own, there was still a shimmering trace of her taste on his mouth, an unfamiliar twinge in his chest. He rather liked it. Smiling as a shiver raced up his spine, Hawk switched on the engine and drove back to the hotel he'd booked on the Vegas Strip.

Not twenty minutes after leaving his car

key with the valet, Hawk was in bed, lost in fantasies of Kate, her lithe, equally naked form close to his.

Hawk woke suddenly, his skin chilled beneath a fine film of perspiration. He was cold, hot and frustrated. He hadn't even realized he'd fallen asleep, only to suddenly awaken right at the most intense part of his fantasy dream. He was aching with need.

Knowing he had to take drastic measures to cool the passion pouring through him, he dragged his body from the bed and headed for the bathroom.

Damn, he hated cold showers.

Kate stood at a side window, one hand flicking the curtain aside an inch or so. Gliding her tongue over her lips, she watched until she could no longer see the car.

She could taste him.

Ridiculous, Kate told herself and let the curtain fall back into place. That mere brush of his mouth over hers had been the furthest thing from a kiss she had ever experienced. She walked to the bedroom. Why in the world would she think she could taste him? Testing, she again slid her tongue along her bottom lip and snivelled.

No, it wasn't ridiculous; she really could taste him, and she liked the taste very much. Kate feared that a real deep kiss from Hawk could very likely be addictive…like rich dark chocolate.

A real deep kiss from Hawk. She replayed the thought inside her head. Swallowing to moisten her suddenly parched throat, she began to undress, her hands fumbling with the simple routine. She mumbled a mild curse to herself.

She had just managed to remove her blouse when the phone rang.

Hawk? Kate froze, her heart beating wildly. It rang again. Not bothering to look at the caller ID, she snatched it up, nearly dropping it. Drawing a quick breath in an attempt to keep a tremor from her voice, she said, "Hello."

"Who was he?" Jeff snarled.

Kate went cold and stiff. "That is none of your business." She wouldn't so much as say his name.

"Yes, it is," he snapped back at her. "You're mine and you know it."

"I never was yours," she said icily. "And I broke up with you months ago, as you well know."

"You were in a snit." He was back to the snarl. "And—"

"No," she said, cutting him off. "You were

being verbally and emotionally abusive... again."

"I'm not giving up, Kate. I know you love me." His voice was suddenly soft, cajoling, "I'll get you back."

"I've been patient up until now, Jeff," she stated flatly, finally saying his name, anger stirring in her voice. "If you bother me again, I'll report you to the police. And this time I mean it."

"Sure," he said in honeyed tones. "You mean it every time, which only tells me you don't mean it."

Kate drew a deep breath in an attempt to control her anger. How in the world had she ever thought that syrupy tone was attractive? Now it repulsed her. *He* repulsed her.

"I have only three words for you, Jeff," she began.

"Yeah, I know," he replied smoothly, interrupting her. "Like I told you, you love me."

"Go to hell." She hung up on him.

Kate stood trembling, staring warily at the phone as if it might attack her.

Damn him. Damn him. Damn him.

She had had enough. Tomorrow morning she would see a lawyer about reporting him to the authorities and would take out a restraining order against him.

Although Kate had never done so before, in case there happened to be an emergency in her family, she was so uneasy that she disconnected the landline and turned off her cell.

After she was ready for bed, she still felt shaken by the call and so she checked the locks on the front door, even though no one could go beyond the lobby without a card key. Then she double-checked the locks on the patio door and on every window.

Kate lay in bed for some time, unable to sleep. When she finally drifted off, she drifted right into a dream. Not of Jeff and fear, but of Hawk and unbelievable pleasure.

He came to her softly, murmuring of the exciting delights to be found in the joining of their bodies. She sighed in her sleep, her body moving in sensual restlessness.

She wanted, needed, ached for his touch, the feel of his mouth taking passionate control of hers, for his hard body possessing, owning, her own.

Kate woke, trembling, quivering deep inside her body, her breathing harsh and uneven. She kicked the covers away from her perspiration-slicked body. Never had she had a dream so real, so vivid that it actually brought her close to release in her sleep.

Her breathing slowly returning to normal, she sat up, staring into the dimness of her bedroom, her mind and senses still reeling.

While it was true that it had been some time since she had been intimate with a man—she would not think his name—it seemed unreal to Kate that a dream of a man she had so recently met and knew practically nothing about, not simply a dream of a fantasy man, could affect her to her very core. Her thoughts ebbed as sleep claimed her once more.

To her surprise, Kate woke later refreshed, if still a bit anxious.

What was with her, anyway? Kate asked herself, musing on her unusual reaction to Hawk. Yes, he was extremely attractive and fun to be with, not to mention sexy as hell. But he was just another man…wasn't he?

Shying away from the thought, Kate centered her attention on the business at hand. Going to the phone, she reconnected the landline and dialed Vic's home number.

Lisa was happy to oblige with the name of a good attorney, as she had been after Kate to swear out a restraining order against Jeff ever since Kate had thrown him out of her apartment.

Minutes later, Kate had an appointment for the next morning with the attorney Lisa had recommended, an older-sounding man named Edward Bender. It was a start.

Four

Even though she knew the time of Hawk's arrival, Kate jumped when the buzzer rang from the intercom in the lobby. Fortunately she had just finished swiping her lashes with the mascara wand, or she would have had a very strange black streak across her temple.

Grabbing her purse and a Black Watch plaid wrap that complemented her off-white dress, she flipped the button and spoke into the wall-mounted receiver.

"Hawk?"

"Yes." His sexy, low voice gave her an all over tingly sensation.

"I'm coming right down."

Without waiting for a response, Kate switched on a night light, locked the door and headed for the elevator.

She had felt an attraction to him from the moment he had walked into Vic's, standing there all tall and lean and ruggedly masculine.

On the other hand, even from the beginning Jeff had appeared almost too handsome, cultured and charming. Almost too good to be true. Of course, before long, his real character had come through.

Kate snorted derisively as she pressed the

elevator button. Handsome, cultured and charming was an act hiding Jeff's true nature.

As Kate stepped inside the elevator, an old adage of her mother's came to mind. *Handsome is as handsome does.* Well, for Kate, handsome had proved to be a nasty jerk when things didn't go exactly the way he wanted them to go.

"Hi," Hawk said as the elevator doors parted. "You look lovely." His eyes held a teasing gleam. "How did you know the Black Watch was my favorite of the clan plaids?"

Kate laughed. "I didn't. It just happens to be my favorite, too. And hello yourself." She grinned.

"Where are we going this evening?"

Shaking his head, Hawk cupped her elbow and led her to the car. "I thought we'd pick up where we were, before we were so rudely interrupted. Do you avoid all casinos or just the one we almost went in last night?"

"Just that one," she said and buckled her seat belt. "But I don't go to casinos very often." She smiled. "As the old song goes, I work hard for my money. But I do play occasionally."

"Table games?" He arched his brows.

"No, I play the machines only." Kate arched her brows back at him. "What about you?"

"Poker, Texas hold 'em," he answered, shrugging. "And some blackjack now and again. Ready to go?"

"Whenever you are," Kate said, and he pulled out of the lot.

He was quiet for a moment as they drove. "I don't know what scent you're wearing but I like it…a lot."

Kate grew warmer and more tingly. "Thank you, Hawk. It's the only scent I wear."

"Whenever or wherever I smell it, I'll think of you." He flashed a smile at her.

Kate was certain everything inside her was melting. She told herself she had better be careful, because this man wasn't merely dangerous, but he was dynamite. Compared to Hawk, she thought, Jeff wasn't even a firecracker.

Playing with firecrackers was one thing, but playing with dynamite… Kate shivered.

"Are you cold?" Hawk asked, noticing her shiver even though he never took his eyes from the road. "I can turn on the car heater." He reached to do so.

"No…no." Kate shook her head while offering a weak smile. "I'm fine, really, and we're almost to the strip." Jeez, she thought, if he turned on the heater, she'd melt right there in front of him.

"It does seem strange," he said. "In October here in Vegas in the afternoon, the temp can go into the seventies and even the eighties, yet in the evening it can drop down into the fifties and forties."

"It's different where you live?" she said, wanting to know every little thing about him, about his life.

He grinned. "It depends what part of the state you're in. In Denver it can get very warm during the day and cooler in the evenings. But in the mountains where I live, while we might get some warmth in the daytime, it can get damned cold at night."

"I like the mountains," she said, unaware of the wistful note in her voice.

"You're not from here originally?"

"No." She shook her head. "I'm from

Virginia, near the Blue Ridge Mountains. My father runs a small horse farm."

He slanted a quick smile at her. "There you go. We have something in common."

"Horses?" She laughed.

"Hey, don't knock it. It's a start."

Kate couldn't help wondering exactly what he meant by a start. A start of what? He was only going to be in Vegas for a while, wasn't he?

Hawk surprised her by avoiding the Strip, driving to one of the older hotel casinos in town, one she had never been inside before. That is, old in comparison to the unbelievably expensive palaces forever under construction.

Kate liked it even better than the much more elaborate pleasure palaces with which Vegas abounded. For one thing, it wasn't nearly as crowded as the others.

"So," Hawk said, "what do you want to do?"

Kate was quiet a moment, glancing around her. "I think I'll wander around a bit—" she flashed a smile at him "—until one of the machines calls to me."

"Fine," he said. He paused before adding, "I think I'll wander to a blackjack table. Suppose we synchronize our watches and meet right here in, say, an hour?"

Grinning, Kate looked at her wristwatch. "Right. If I don't see you before, I'll see you then."

They had no sooner separated than Kate began to feel lonely. Silly, she chided herself, checking out the lines of machines as she strolled around.

In a bid to distract herself from thoughts of Hawk, she sat down at a machine at the end of a row. She spent several minutes studying the instructions on the three-coin machine before feeding a twenty into the money slot. She racked up eighty credits in the credit window.

Kate had played the machine for almost the full hour when she became aware that someone new had taken the machine beside her. She did not spare a glance at the person.

"Hello, Kate." Jeff's smooth voice gave her a start. "I saw you sitting here all alone and came to keep you company."

Jeff, here? Kate could hardly believe it. This casino was not the kind he frequented; he preferred the glitzy new ones that drew all the celebrities. The thought that followed sent a chill down her spine.

Was he following her, stalking her?

Scared but determined not to reveal her fear

to him, Kate turned a cold look on him. "I'm not alone. I have company, and even if I didn't, I would never want yours."

"Now, Kate, we both know you don't—"

That was as far as she allowed him to go. "You know nothing, Jeff, but I'll enlighten you." She drew courage from the cool tones she had achieved. "If you aren't gone from my sight within the next few seconds, I will begin screaming for security."

"You wouldn't dare," he said. "You forget I know you hate making a scene."

"Perhaps," she admitted, "but I'll gladly make an exception in your case." She made a show of glancing at her watch. "You have exactly two seconds to disappear." She didn't look away from her watch. "One…two…"

He was off the stool and moving away from her, swearing a blue streak. Shaken by the encounter, she drew a calming breath, and the minute he was out of her sight, she hit the pay-out button and walked away with five dollars more than she'd started with.

She was hurrying back to the place where she'd agreed to meet Hawk when she spotted him at a blackjack table. She hesitated a moment but then decided to approach him, certain Jeff wouldn't try anything again so long as Hawk was near.

Coming up behind him, Kate laid a hand on his shoulder to let him know she was there. "Hi. I see you're winning." There were several stacks of chips in front of him.

"Yeah." He turned to smile at her. "You ready to leave?"

"No hurry," she said. "I'd like to watch awhile, if you don't mind me standing in back of you as you play."

"Not at all," he said, managing to keep an eye on the play of cards at the same time. "I'm not superstitious. Fact is, I like you there."

Feeling inordinately pleased and warmed by his comment, especially after that unpleasant encounter with Jeff, Kate lightly flexed her fingers on his shoulder. The warmth flowed stronger when he raised a hand to cover hers briefly, his fingers lacing with hers.

The feeling of his touch remained on her even as the evening continued. Would his touch bring such torrid dreams again? She hoped it would banish those nightmares that only Jeff could inspire.

Five

The idea was to tire himself out enough to sleep. Hawk knew that was the only reason he found himself back at the poker tables until after two in the morning. As he had earlier in the evening, he won. But that wasn't the purpose.

He didn't even doze off, not until after four. Hell, he thought, prowling around the spacious room, popping the top off a can of light beer, he might as well have stayed at the poker tables. He stopped at the floor-to-ceiling window to stare at the glaringly bright lights along the Strip. On the street below, the traffic, both human and vehicular, was almost as heavy as in the afternoon or evening. He took a swig of the cold beer. Obviously there was more than one town in the country that never slept.

His thoughts swirled continuously, every one about Kate. Hawk sighed, "Kate." He didn't realize he had whispered her name aloud or finished off the beer. Shaking his head at his wandering mind, he tossed the can into the wastebasket.

He wanted to be with her so badly, he ached with the wanting, the raw need. His back teeth hurt from clenching them together. There were other women in Vegas; there had been plenty of them in the casino and the restaurant yesterday morning. Several of them had cast unmistakable looks of availability at him. He had ignored them.

Just any woman wouldn't do. Hawk was always selective when it came to the females he spent time with, despite the fact that he so seldom left the ranch.

This time around was different. Hawk was coming to the reluctant conclusion that the only woman he wanted to spend his time with was Kate.

And Kate had man problems, dammit.

She appeared to resent the oily guy more than fear him...but one could never really know what another person was thinking, feeling. Vic had said Kate had thrown the creep out of her apartment for verbally abusing her. And last night he had been far from pleasant.

Hawk frowned. Was the jerk harassing her? Had he been harassing her since she dumped him? Hell, that was months ago now.

When Kate had joined him at the black-jack table earlier that night, she had seemed different than when they had separated, he to play the tables and she to play the slots. It had been nothing overt or obvious. She had been quieter and slightly more reserved, not at all the woman who had laughed so easily earlier.

The wheels in Hawk's mind were rolling full speed. Had that creep approached her again between the time they parted and when she joined him at the blackjack table? Had she come to him for protection? Hmm, it was possible, and now that he thought about it, probable.

Confused by her sudden change in mood,

he had slightly withdrawn. He had had such high hopes for a kiss, a real kiss, with her before she went into her apartment building.

Hope in one hand and spit in the other.

The old saying of his father's slipped through his mind. Hawk rejected the very idea that he gave up hope. Sliding beneath the covers again, he thought he had better get some sleep if he wanted to be sharp enough to catch any slight change in her attitude, because he *could* see her tomorrow.

This time he was unconscious within minutes.

Kate entered Mr. Bender's office with a heavy step that morning. The lawyer was older—close to sixty she judged—and he appeared to be the classic prototype of an old-fashioned gentleman.

She told him her problem. In turn, Mr. Bender had questions.

"Did he ever hit you, even the lightest slap?"

"No." Kate shook her head. "But…I must admit there were times when he was the most angry, swearing…I began fearing he might."

"I see. Did he ever threaten you?"

"Not outright," she said, "but in a vague, oblique way." She sighed. "I don't know how else to describe it, but he frightens me."

"Now, don't you worry, Miss Muldoon. The law will take care of this…" He hesitated, his lips pursed as if from a sour taste. "This lowlife."

Sighing with resignation at her predicament, Kate pushed herself through the revolving door.

Directly into reality. Her cell phone rang.

Kate hesitated, eyeing the instrument as if it might leap into the air and bite her. It wasn't a number she recognized.

Thoughts whipped through her head, one tripping over another. Jeff…the bastard. She knew; she knew he'd track her to the lawyer's. He must have followed her.

What to do?

The phone rang for the third time. Kate opened the phone, determining to rip a verbal strip off him.

"Hello?" Her mouth was bone-dry; her voice, sharp with impatience. She fully expected to hear Jeff's angry voice in response.

"Kate?"

A silent sigh of relief slipped through her lips. "Hawk! I, uh, I'm glad to hear it's you. I had a lovely time last night," she said, trying to forget the unwanted and unwelcome appearance of Jeff, and the doubts assailing her now.

"I'm glad." Now she could hear the relief in his voice. "I wondered whether something had upset you."

"Well, you wondered wrong," she said, her tone firm. "It's been a very long time since I laughed the way I have with you these past two evenings, Hawk. It felt good." Too good.

In all honesty, and as much as she would have liked to deny it, she felt shaky at the awareness it was him on the line. She felt as if everything was smoldering inside her—and breathless, shivery. She had felt somewhat the same at first with Jeff almost two years ago. This time the feeling was stronger, more intense. No, she didn't like it at all.

She had believed herself immune to any other charmer. For Jeff had been charming and gallant for many months, right up until she had agreed to him moving in with her, his ring on her finger. For a while she had been content. Her contentment had lasted all of three months. A bitter taste filled her mouth. First Jeff had become possessive, questioning her every move when they weren't together. Then he had become verbally abusive, cursing, accusing her of being with other men, even Vic.

The warm sensations that had been inside Kate faded to cold determination. She could not, would not, go through a situation like that again.

He jumped on her last remark. "In that case, lunch?"

She had no choice but to smile, and it did feel good, dammit. And she couldn't resist, didn't want to resist, even though she feared she'd regret it.

"I've got to stop by my apartment to change. Do you want to meet me there?"

"Sure. What time?"

Kate glanced at her wristwatch, noting it was not quite twelve-thirty. "Would forty-five minutes work? You realize I'm not going to even ask whether Vic gave you the number."

He chuckled in reply. "See you then."

Within fifteen minutes, Kate was entering her apartment. Slipping off her jacket as she went, she headed for her bedroom. She removed the rest of her suit, hung it back in the closet and made a beeline for the bathroom, wanting to wash up before applying fresh makeup.

She smoothed her hair with a brush, giving

it a healthy sheen. Makeup was fast and easy. She kept it light, natural looking. Back in the bedroom she was reaching into the closet for one of the outfits she wore only to work when the buzzer sounded on the intercom.

Hawk? Kate shot a look at the bedside clock. Only thirty-five minutes had passed since she'd talked to him. Pulling on a light-weight robe, she went running to the intercom.

"Yes?" she said on a quick breath.

"Ready for lunch?"

A flutter tickled her stomach, clutched at her throat. "Err…" she said, "not quite. Sorry."

"That's okay, I'll wait."

"You don't have to wait in the lobby," she said, feeling uncertain that inviting him up was wise. Still, she did. "I'll buzz the lock on the lobby door. I'm in the second-floor front apartment. Just walk in. I'll be ready in a few minutes."

"Gotcha."

That was what she was afraid of, and if he did have her, what did he intend to do with her?

Thinking she must either be nuts or self-destructive, Kate unlocked the front door and, turning, dashed back into her bedroom, shutting the door behind her.

She heard the front door open and Hawk call out, "I'm here, Kate. Take your time. I'm in no hurry."

In the process of fastening her belt, Kate had to smile. Hawk was—or at least appeared to be—so nice, pleasant. But then appearances, she reminded herself, were deceiving. She sighed, fully aware that she knew that better than most.

When she entered the living room, Hawk was standing with his back to her, perusing the books on her five-shelf bookcase. He looked gorgeous from the rear.

"See something you like?" she asked, her face growing warm from merely thinking about his tight rear.

He turned to smile at her before replying. "Now I do." He ran a slow look over her, which parched her throat and moistened other places she didn't care to think about at the moment.

"Ready to go?" she asked brightly, perhaps a bit too brightly.

"Ready for anything," he said in a tone that was darn close to a purr. "What about you?"

So am I. The thought zapped into her mind and she immediately zapped it back out. "Uhh..." She stalled, trying to think of a reply, then improvised. "Well, if you don't mind, I'm not ready for lunch…at least not in a restaurant." She dragged up a facsimile of a smile. "I'll be spending most of the rest of the day in a restaurant."

He shrugged. "Okay, what would you rather do?"

She didn't have to think about that one. "It's such a mild and beautiful day. "I'd like to spend some time outside. What do you think?" Kate watched as he pondered her suggestion for all of a few seconds.

"I think it's a great idea," he said and arched one brow. "Do you like hot dogs?"

Kate had to smile. "I love hot dogs, especially dogs loaded with chili."

"Well…" he said slowly, "how about we drive to town, park and stroll around the outside of the casino hotels. Some of the grounds are beautiful. When we're ready, we can go into one of the hotel food courts, have our dogs and, if we still have time, maybe check out some of the upscale shops."

Kate came to a halt, staring at him as if he had two heads.

"What?" Hawk said, frowning.

"You like to shop?" She managed a fake note of awe.

His frown turned into a wry expression. "I wouldn't go so far as to say I like it, but I don't mind shopping occasionally…like two or three times a year." He grinned at her.

Even as she shook her head in despair at him, Kate grinned back. "Okay. Let's roll before you change your mind."

"Good idea." As if unconscious of his move, Hawk curled his hand around hers, laced their fingers together and led them out the door.

Kate's hand tingled with warmth as they rode the elevator to the ground floor. When the doors slid apart, she immediately felt both chilled and angry all over at the sight that met her eyes.

Jeff… What was he doing there? Her earlier fear coursed back. She could hardly miss his hand reaching for the buzzer to one of the apartments. She felt Hawk stiffen beside her, as if readying for a fight, either verbal or physical.

"What are you doing here, Jeff?" she said, trying to tell Hawk to keep his cool by squeezing his hand.

Without taking his hard-eyed gaze off Jeff, Hawk tightened his grip on her fingers.

"I came to invite you to brunch," Jeff answered, his tone of voice demeaning. "But I see you obviously have already eaten."

Steel infused Kate's back and her head lifted, propelled by pride and anger at the insult in his double entendre. A low, almost growling sound in his throat, Hawk took a step forward.

"Don't," she said, yanking his hand to hold him back. "He's not worth your time and energy." She looked at Jeff with distaste. "I saw a lawyer today. He is going to swear out an order of restraint against you."

"You bitch," Jeff snarled. "And you think that should worry me?" His laugh was harsh, demeaning. "I should have taught you who's boss long ago."

Kate felt the simmering anger inside Hawk with the tremor that flashed through him from his rough hand in hers.

"You gutless bastard." Hawk's voice was very soft, controlled and somehow terrifying. He again took a step forward, loosening his fingers to draw his hand away from hers.

Kate clasped his arm with her free hand, holding him in place next to her.

"I'd advise you to leave, Jeff, while you are still in one piece," Hawk growled.

Though Jeff sneered and put on an act of bravado, as if unimpressed with the six-foot-six-inch Hawk, he cast a disparaging look at Kate as he turned, yanked open the lobby door, then paused to glance back this time in clear fear and anger. He glared at Hawk. "You have no idea the trouble you're going to be in." He sneered. "I have friends in this town."

"Yeah, yeah," Hawk drawled, obviously neither impressed nor intimidated. "And all of them in low places, I'm sure. You know what you can do with your threats and your friends. Get lost."

His face looking like it was about to cave in

on itself, Jeff tore out of the lobby. The swiftness of his steps as he headed for his car was proof that the bigger man had more than intimidated him. He had scared the hell out of him.

"Son of a bitch," Hawk said softly between his teeth, harsh anger in his voice. Tension hummed through his taut body. He made another move, as if to follow after Jeff.

"Hawk, please don't," Kate said, tugging his hand.

He paused, but his hard-eyed gaze remained fixed on the other man until he drove away. Only then did he shift his gaze to her. "I'm not a violent man, Kate," he said, his voice still threaded with anger. "But I'll take only so much, be pushed only so far…."

"Not today," she said, smiling in hopes of cooling his temper.

"No?" Hawk raised one brow. "Says who?"

The tension and anger were gone; his eyes teased her.

"Me…I…" She shook her head. "Whatever. I'm ready for a walk in the sunshine… I need a breath of fresh air after that nasty encounter."

Hawk's expression was sober, but his eyes continued to tease. "Okay, but this jaunt better be good."

"Or?" Kate asked in challenge.

"Or it won't be," he said, grinning, an invitation for her to join him.

Her relief palpable, Kate laughed.

The tension gone, they had a brief tug-of-war over whose car they were going to use. Hawk won with the simple offer to drop Kate off at work afterward.

The hours they spent together seemed to fly by. They talked practically the entire time, except while they were devouring the chili dogs, sharing one order of French fries and sipping on iced tea.

In a boutique in the Forum Shops at Caesars, they discussed the array of colorful cashmere scarves since Hawk was considering giving one as a Christmas gift to his sister, Catriona. Kate didn't hesitate giving him her opinion.

"This is beautiful. Perfect for winter," she said, holding up a scarf in swirling shades of forest green, russet and antique gold.

His lean fingers lightly stroked the length of the soft material.

As if he were touching her, a tingle slid the length of Kate's spine in time with the stroking of his fingers. She drew a quick breath before asking, "Yes? No?"

He nodded. "I think you're right. "It's

perfect. Is there anything else you want to look at?"

"No." She shook her head.

"You wouldn't like one of these scarves for yourself?"

"I'd love one," she said ruefully. "But my clothing budget doesn't stretch to cashmere anything."

From the expression that flittered over his face, Kate was afraid for a moment that he was going to offer to buy her one of the gorgeous scarves. She softly sighed with relief when he shrugged.

"Are you ready to go, then?"

"Yes," she said, glad he hadn't made an offer she would have to refuse, even one involving a simple, if very expensive item.

Kate was happy to get outside again and barely noticed where they were walking until they were in sight of where Hawk had parked the car. It was only then that she glanced at her watch for the first time since they had left her apartment complex.

An odd sensation, almost like sadness, settled on her as they drove to Vic's restaurant. Their day together was almost over. Kate doubted there would ever be another one, as he would soon be leaving for his ranch, his vacation over.

"I had a lovely day, Hawk. Thank you," she said when he brought the car to a stop in the restaurant lot. This time she waited until he opened the car door for her.

"You're welcome, Kate." His hand on the door handle, Hawk looked at her as she emerged from the car, an endearingly soft smile curving his tempting mouth. He leaned toward her. Without a thought, she met him halfway.

Hawk's kiss was as soft as his smile and gentle, with no sudden hungry pressure or demand.

Naturally, Kate wanted more, a lot more. Obviously, Hawk did, too. A low groan of protest slipped into her mouth as he reluctantly drew away.

Moving back, away from her, he dragged a deep breath into his body. Looking her straight in the eyes, he said, simply, "When?"

Kate didn't need to question him. She knew exactly what he meant. The heat radiating through her body was a dead giveaway. He wanted her. Always honest with herself, she acknowledged she wanted him just as badly. But… Why did there always have to be a but? Nevertheless, there it was. Feeling she had known him forever didn't change the fact that she had met Hawk less than a week ago, and she didn't really know the inner man, the un-varnished person.

Oh, Kate was well aware that there were women who "hooked up" with a man the same day or night of meeting him. Yet as hackneyed as it sounded, she was not one of those women.

"Kate?"

At the soft sound of his voice, Kate blinked to meet his direct stare.

"I'm sorry, Hawk," she said, disappoint-ment tingeing her tone. "I...I'm just not sure...I..."

"Shh," he soothed, raising a hand to glide a finger along the curve of her cheek. "It's all right. I can wait." A self-deprecating smile played over his lips. "Well, I think I can wait." His smile turned teasing as he added, "I'll suffer in silent agony."

Kate had to laugh, but she felt like crying. "You really don't need to come back for me tonight. Vic will drive me home."

There it was, her feeble declaration of independence. Hawk stared at her for a moment, but she knew he had understood. She was feeling pressured and was asking him to give her some room.

He gave her a wry smile and circled the car to the driver's side. "May I call you tonight, after you get home from work?"

"Yes, of course." She glanced at her watch. "I've got to go, Hawk, or I'll be late."

"Tonight," he said, standing by the open car door.

"Tonight," she echoed, softly sighing as he slid behind the wheel and swung the door shut.

Kate made it to Vic's just in time, not that

Vic would have said anything if she had been a few minutes late. While he was easygoing—the employees didn't even have to clock in—she was a nut about punctuality. Although she admitted she had plenty of human flaws, being late wasn't one of them.

Big deal, Kate thought, hanging her jacket on the coat rack in the employees' break room. So she was never, or hardly ever, late for anything. What was so great about that? She would be better served by being tough rather than prompt. If she were tough, she would have had Jeff hauled into court for abuse and harassment long ago.

But, no, she hadn't done that. She had tried reasoning with him. Ha! A lot that had got her. She should have realized early on that there was simply no reasoning with the self-indulgent, narcissistic jerk.

And Kate knew Jeff would ignore any restraining order and would do exactly as he pleased, which meant the continued harassment of her, especially after Hawk returned home.

There was only one thing she could do. Though Kate had thought of it many times, she now felt certain she had to leave Vegas. She had put off the decision because she liked it here, liked her job and the people she worked with. And she loved Vic, Lisa and Bella like family.

No, as much as she wanted to stay, she couldn't take a chance of putting her friends in danger. Kate heaved a sigh of regret and hurried to the hostess station to relieve the older woman who worked part-time handling the lunch patrons.

She was afraid the day would drag by. It didn't. The restaurant was so busy, time just flew. Kate also expected Hawk to amble in for dinner. He didn't. So, of course, not only was she disappointed, but she couldn't help but wonder where and with whom he might be spending his evening.

After they closed the restaurant, Vic walked Kate to his car. "Are you all right, Kate?" he asked, sounding concerned. "You've been awful quiet tonight."

"I'm fine," she answered, managing a smile for him. "At least I will be after tomorrow."

Vic frowned, opening the car door for her. "What's happening then?"

Kate sighed. "Jeff's been bothering me again," she said, touching his arm reassuringly when she saw him grow stiff. "It's all right, Vic. Nothing happened. Hawk was with me at the time."

Vic cocked an eyebrow. "And nothing happened? Hawk didn't do anything?"

She smiled, if faintly, looking at her hand on his arm. "He couldn't. I held him back."

Vic actually laughed. "Yeah, right. Honey, if Hawk wanted to go for him, you wouldn't have been able to hold him back."

"I said please." She gave him a sweet smile and fluttered her eyelashes at him.

"Yeah." Vic nodded. "I can see that would have stopped even Hawk." Shaking his head, he ushered her into the car. Although she knew he was bursting with questions, Vic didn't voice even one as he drove her home.

She had no sooner entered her apartment than the phone rang. Hawk. Dropping her purse onto a chair, she hurried to the phone and snatched it up.

Six

"Hello?" Somehow she managed to keep her voice calm, concealing the eagerness she felt.

"I'm sorry, Kate."

She froze, hand gripping the receiver. "I won't speak to you, Jeff."

Before she could hang up on him, he went on. "Please, Kate, listen. I mean it. I'm so sorry for what I said to you today in the lobby. I was just so shocked to see you step out of the elevator with that man, I…" He paused as if to catch his breath.

Kate frowned. He had made an odd noise. Was he crying? Jeff? Ha! Was she crazy?

He babbled on. "Baby, I can't—"

"I told you before, over and over again, not to call me that," she said, cutting him off.

"I know, and I'm sorry. I forgot. Geez, Kate, I love you so much, I can't stand it."

"Jeff. Restraining order," she said, striving for patience. "I have nothing to say to you except leave me alone."

"Damn you, Kate!"

The call waiting signal beeped. Relief washed through her.

Hawk.

She had to get rid of Jeff. "I have another call. I'm going to hang up."

"*Kate*, you will be *very* sor—" Kate pressed

the flashing button. Drawing a quick steadying breath, she said, "Hello?"

"Hi." His voice was soft, intimate.

Shivering in reaction to the nasty note in Jeff's voice, Kate dropped onto the chair beside the phone table and curled into herself, trying to contain the shakes. "Hi, yourself," she said as calmly as possible. "Have a nice evening?"

"You want the polite answer or the truth?"

She dredged up a quivering smile. "The truth." Or maybe not, she thought, but it was too late to change her mind.

"Well…" He exhaled a very long sigh. "I ate dinner…alone. I went to the pool…alone. I played some poker. I won…alone." He sighed again, so sad and forlorn. "I took a nap…alone." That last comment was followed by a groan.

Kate was holding her hand over her

mouth to keep from laughing—or was it sobbing?—out loud.

He went on. "I had a late snack...alone. I played blackjack...alone." Now, as if he was having difficulty controlling his voice, a sliver of humor broke through. He cleared his throat. "I won again...alone. You get the picture?"

She opened her mouth.

He didn't wait for an answer. "Dammit, Kate, I was missing you like hell the whole time."

Kate couldn't hold it in any longer; instead of sobs, laughter poured out of her.

"Sure, you can laugh," Hawk groused, very close to chuckling. "You had friends and customers around all day and evening to talk to. You were probably even flirting with some of those nice old gentlemen I've noticed watching you as you walk away from the tables."

"What?" Kate blinked. Confusion overrode a lingering fear. "What are you talking about?" She drew an easier breath. "What nice old gentlemen?"

"The ones with the nice old ladies who aren't paying attention," he shot back at her, pausing before clarifying. "I mean, those regular patrons I've seen there every time I've been there."

"The regular old gentlemen customers watch me walk away from their tables?" How funny, she mused. She really hadn't known.

"Sure they do," he answered. "The younger men do, too, when their dates or wives aren't paying attention." He gave a short laugh. "I've been sending quite a few glares their way."

"Really?" she asked, pleased and surprised. "Why?"

"I had rather hoped I was the only one
watching the gentle, sensuous sway of your
hips," he murmured.

Oh my. Kate grew warm—no, hot—all
over. She drew a deep, silent breath and let it
out softly, all thoughts of Jeff banished.

"Kate?"

"Yes, Hawk?" Her voice was little more
than a whisper of air through her suddenly dry
lips.

"When?"

She swallowed to moisten her dry throat
and took a look at her watch. "Hawk, it's
nearly one o'clock in the morning."

"Yeah, I know…and I'm starving."

For you.

He didn't need to say it. Kate heard it loud

and clear. Not allowing herself to hesitate, consider, she murmured, "I am, too, Hawk." Starving and scared.

"So?" His voice was quiet, calm, without a hint of pressure.

Kate wet her lips, swallowed again and said, "How soon can you get here?"

"Twenty-five minutes or so, maybe less if the traffic has thinned," he responded at once, sexual electricity sizzling in his tone.

"I'll be counting the minutes."

"I'm on my way." He hung up.

Determined to push Jeff's not-so-veiled threats from her mind, Kate replaced the receiver and disconnected the phone cord from the wall jack. Digging her cell phone out of her purse, she turned that off, too, before rising to go into her bedroom.

Hawk had said around twenty-five minutes

or so. That was just enough time for her to have a quick shower and slip into something a little more comfortable. Simply thinking about that made her smile as she undressed and headed for the bathroom. Tossing off her clothes, she stepped into the shower, careful not to get her hair wet.

Kate was excited but nervous, as well. She hadn't been with a man in some time, and in all truth, she had never thought the act of sex was the end all and be all it was made out to be.

What if she disappointed Hawk? On the other hand, what if he disappointed her? An image of him swam into her mind. Somehow she doubted he could disappoint any woman.

Why was she taking this course now, with this particular man? She had had offers before, many times. Why Hawk? Oh, sure, he was very attractive, masculine and made her laugh.

He made her feel safe and secure.

Was that enough reason to go to bed with a man? They were practically strangers…and yet. Kate shook the thoughts away as she stepped out of the shower and stuffed the wet towel and her clothing into the wicker laundry basket in the closet.

Why was she analyzing her reasons? She was thirty-one years old; she didn't need reasons to go to bed with a man. What she needed was the man, this man, simply because he turned her on something fierce.

She opened a dresser drawer and reached for a nightshirt. No. Why bother? she thought, slipping into her silk, wide-sleeved, knee-length robe. If you're going to do it, do it right, she told herself, staring into the mirror to smooth her hair.

Makeup? Kate shook her head. No. No

artifice. This was the way she looked. It was take it or leave it, Mr. Hawk McKenna.

The intercom buzzed. Kate froze, frowning at her reflection. Maybe she should quickly apply a bit of makeup, if only blush.

No. No backing out, she thought, backing away from the dresser and walking to her bedroom doorway. Drawing a deep breath, she rushed to the intercom to buzz Hawk through the lobby door.

The next instant she nearly panicked. Good grief! What if it wasn't Hawk? What if it was Jeff, coming to back his threats up physically?

The doorbell rang. Standing rigid, Kate said softly, "Hawk?"

His answer came back as softly. "Who were you expecting? The big bad wolf?"

Close, she thought. Dragging a smile to her

lips, she unlocked the door and opened it for him, one brow arched. "Aren't you? The big bad wolf, I mean." Swinging the door open wide, she moved back.

Stepping inside, he shut the door, locked it, tossed aside the windbreaker he carried and stood there, leaning back against the door frame. His heated gaze took note of every inch of her body. "I wish I were," he murmured, closing the short distance between them. "You certainly look good enough to eat."

"Hmm…uh…would you like something to drink?" Her throat was dry; her voice low, raspy.

His mouth took hers, ending her question. His kiss was every bit as soft, gentle and un-demanding as before…for a moment. With a soft growl deep in his throat, Hawk parted her lips with his tongue, delving, tasting every part of her mouth before plunging deep inside.

Afraid her legs would fail her, Kate grasped him at the waist, hanging on for dear life. His kiss was hot, devastating. Drowning in sensations, she slid her hands up his chest and curled her arms around his neck.

Without releasing her mouth, Hawk slowly rose to his full height, taking her with him. Her feet dangling a foot or so off the floor, he carried her into the bedroom, closing the door with a backward thrust of one foot.

Still he held her lips and her mind in thrall as he lowered one hand to the base of her spine, drawing her hips in line with his own.

Hawk's purpose was apparent and successful. Kate felt the hard fullness of him. Lost in the fiery world of sensuality, needy and wanting, she held her hips tightly to him.

"I know," he said at her sudden movement, ending the kiss to allow them both to breathe, pressing into her body.

Kate drew a deep breath before trying to speak. "What do you think we should do about it?" she said, surprising herself with her brazen response to him. Never before had she felt like this, and certainly never with…oh, the hell with *him*. He was a nothing compared to Hawk. No, he was a nothing, period.

"I suppose I could think of a few things," he drawled, his lips a hair's breadth from hers. "We could start with losing our clothes." His tongue tickled the corner of her mouth.

She hadn't known a touch so simple could cause such a burning reaction. Kate couldn't wait to find out what else she hadn't known. Eager to learn, she cupped his head with her hands, and whispering, "More, please," she roughly drew his mouth to hers.

Hawk was quick to comply. This time his kiss wasn't as long, but it was just as powerful. Breathing deeply, harshly, he murmured, "I'm going to burst out of these jeans if I don't get them off soon."

Having no idea that the smile was seductive, Kate lowered her arms and stepped back, looking directly at the spot he indicated.

"This I want to see," she murmured.

Shoes, socks and pants were removed and kicked aside before he answered.

"Well, I didn't mean literally." His gaze devoured her as he dug into a pocket of the discarded jeans, withdrew a foil packet and laid it on the nightstand.

Kate's breaths were coming out of her body in tiny puffs. Her throat felt parched. Curious, she shamefully lowered her gaze to his boxer shorts, her breathing halting altogether at the sight and size of the bulge there. She tried to swallow, was unable and had to try again. She never even saw him pull off his golf shirt.

"Not fair," he said, his own voice sounding desert dry. "I'm doing all the undressing."

Raising her glance, she gasped for breath at the sight of the width of his flat, muscled chest. She blinked as it and he moved closer. She looked up and immediately down again as he pushed down the boxers and kicked them aside.

Good grief! The man was big, absolutely beautiful in form, and perfectly proportioned. Reluctantly returning her gaze to his face, she found him watching her, as if studying her reaction to his nakedness.

"You're…you're beautiful," she whispered, staring into his smoldering gaze.

"Men aren't beautiful." There was a trace of pleasure in his voice at her compliment.

"Sure they are," she said, a wave of her hand brushing aside his rebuttal. "At least you are." She hesitated a moment before blurting out, "Anyway, *I* think you are."

Hawk stepped up close to her, his hand reaching for the belt of her robe. "I disagree with you, but I confess I did like hearing it." The belt knot loose, he gently parted the sides of her robe to glide a slow look over her body. "Now, that's my definition of beauty." Slipping the silky cloth off her, he let it drop to the floor.

Kate was hot and cold. She was shivering on the surface of her body, but a fire blazing inside.

"Hawk?" It was the only word she could manage from her dry throat. It was enough.

"Anything you want, Kate. Anything," he murmured, throwing back the bedcover and sweeping her into his arms to lay her in the middle of her bed. The next instant he was beside her, drawing her to the heat and hardness of his body.

"Another kiss," she said, moving with him as he flipped onto his back, drawing her over his chest. His hands cradling her face, he slowly drew her lips down to his. His tongue was ready for the meeting of mouths, laving her lower lip, driving her wild for more.

Feeling like a column of flames burning only for him, she shuddered at his intimate exploration of her body...every inch of her body. And all the while he murmured to her about what he would do next, sending her anticipation, excitement and tension higher and higher.

Her breathing as rough as his, moaning softly, Kate matched him kiss for kiss, stroke for stroke, thrilling at the sound of his own deep-throated moans.

"That feels so good," he whispered when at last she took him in her hand, marveling at the thick length of him. "But be careful. Don't go too far."

"Are you sure?" Kate didn't need to ask him what he meant; she knew very well. Still, obeying an impish urge, she wriggled down his now sweat-moistened body and took him into her mouth.

Hawk's body jerked as though he had been touched by a live wire. "Kate...I..." His voice gave way to a groan and he arched into her as she laved him with her tongue. "Damn, Kate. You've got to stop now." His voice was ragged yet his hands were gentle as he grasped her shoulders and pulled her body up the length of his.

"I thought you might like that," she said, the same impish feeling driving her to tease him.

"Like it?" Heaving a deep breath, he rolled both of them over until he was on top of her. "Oh, you have no idea. I loved it."

"But…" she began, enjoying teasing him.

"But I want to be inside you," he said, settling his body between her legs.

Kate sighed as she watched him tear the foil packet, sheath himself. She arched her hips as he slowly, too slowly, slid himself inside her, joining them as one.

Dragging harsh breaths into her chest, Kate sighed with pure pleasure as he began a steady rhythm, slowly building the tension coiling inside her.

Catching him by the hips, she pulled him

deeper inside her quivering body, needing more and more of him until, with a soft cry, the tension snapped, flinging her into a shattering release.

A moment later she heard Hawk exhale a gritted "whoa." And felt the shudder of his body as he exploded within her.

With a heavy sigh, Hawk settled on top of her, his face nestled in the curve of her neck. Drained, satiated, Kate idly stroked his shoulders, his back, and kissed his forehead in thanks for the pleasure he had given to her, a pleasure she had never before experienced.

She sighed with utter contentment.

"Yeah," he said in complete understanding. "That has never happened before. An orgasm as strong as that," he murmured close to her ear, which he proceeded to nibble on. "I thought the top of my head would blow off."

"If it does, you'll clean it up," she said, tilting her head to give him better access to her neck, where he was dropping tiny kisses.

Chuckling, he lifted himself up so he could look down at her. "You're something else. You know that?" Without giving her time to respond, he kissed her in a way that was every bit as hot and arousing as before.

Where did the man get his stamina? Kate wondered hazily. Feeling him growing again against the apex of her thighs, she went warm all over. How was it possible for him to be ready again so soon? she mused, every bit as ready as he was. She moved against the hardness pressing against her.

"More?" he asked, his tone soft and hopeful.

"Oh, yes, please." Kate surprised herself with her immediate and pleading answer.

This time Hawk took his time. Slow and easy, he caressed, stroked, kissed every inch of her, lingering on her breasts with maddening attention.

Moving sensuously against him, moaning low with pleasure, she speared her fingers through his long hair, holding him to her as she arched her back.

"Like that?" he said, flicking his tongue over one tight nipple.

Kate was barely able to speak but she managed to sigh, "Oh, yes." Without warning him, she pushed against him until she could slide out from beneath him.

"What—"

"Shush," she said, turning on her side to face him. "I want to play, too." Leaning against him, she gently kissed one of his flat nipples.

Hawk sucked in a breath, then let it out on a laugh. "I did say we could do anything you want. My body's your playground for the rest of the night."

Gliding one palm down his chest, Kate laughed, too.

"Sounds tempting, but I doubt I'll last that long." Her teasing hand found its destination. "From the size of you, I doubt you can last that long."

Hawk's hand was also moving, curving over her small waist and rounded hips to the apex of her thighs. He drew a quick gasp from her with his exploring fingers.

"Oh my God!" she cried. "Hawk, stop. I can't wait much longer. I want you now."

"That's good." His voice was raw. "Because I can't hold out much longer, either."

Rolling her onto her back, he slid between

her thighs and entered her. Within moments they cried out their release simultaneously.

It took longer this time for Kate to come down from the sexual high. Slowly her breathing returned to normal. She smiled as Hawk flipped onto his back, his breathing still labored.

"That was fantastic," he said, turning his head to grin at her.

Although Kate blushed, she felt a sense of deep satisfaction and just a bit of pride. She felt so very pleased, in fact, that she returned his compliment with complete honesty.

"Know what? I've never, ever experienced anything even vaguely like that." Pleasantly exhausted, she curled up against his warm, moist body and closed her eyes.

"Hey, don't go to sleep on me," he said, sitting up. "Well, you may go to sleep on me, but not until we've cleaned up under a shower."

Kate groaned in protest as he took her by the shoulders to sit her up next to him. "Hawk, please. I don't want a shower. I just want to sleep."

"Oh, c'mon, my Kate," he coaxed, sliding off the bed with her in his arms. "A quick wash, and then you may sleep till it's time to get ready for work tomorrow." Cradling her in his arms, he strode into the bathroom as if he weren't a bit tired.

He let her legs slide to the floor. "You have the silkiest skin," he said, stroking his hands over her shoulders.

"Thank you." Kate shivered with the thrill of his words and his caress. "Can we get a shower now? I'm freezing and still sleepy."

Hawk heaved a deep sigh. "Oh, okay," he

groused, picking her up again and stepping into the shower stall. He turned the water on full blast, and for a few minutes it was very cold.

"Hawk!" she yelped as her shivering intensified.

He wrapped his arms around her shoulders, drew her against his still warm body. "Better?"

She sighed when she felt the heat of him and the warming water. "Much better. Now let's get this over with."

True to his promise of a quick wash, he impersonally soaped and rinsed them both. Picking her up by the waist, he lifted her out of the shower, set her feet down on the shower mat and joined her there.

Kate was the first to dry off. Dashing into the bedroom, she pulled a thigh-length, baseball-style nightshirt from a dresser drawer and slipped into it. She was diving under the rumpled covers as he left the bathroom.

Smiling gently at her, he reached for his boxer shorts and sat on the edge of the bed to put them on. When he grabbed his jeans, she stopped him.

"What are you doing?" she asked.

He slanted a curious look at her, as if his actions should be obvious. "Getting dressed."

"Why?" She frowned.

"Why else?" he answered, frowning back at her. "So you can get the sleep you were whining about."

"I was not whining," she said indignantly. "Anyway, I thought you'd stay, sleep with me." She was beginning to feel hurt and, ridiculously, used.

Hawk went dead still. "You want me to stay the night?" Hope coated his voice.

"Isn't that what I just said?" She smiled.

"You talked me into it." Smiling back, he dropped the jeans to the floor and crawled into the bed, beside her. "I'm sleepy, too." With that he settled, spoon fashion, behind her, smiling when he heard her soft sigh.

Warm and cuddling, they were both asleep within minutes.

Seven

Kate woke, immediately aware of three things: the bed beside her was empty, the clock on the nightstand read 11:42 a.m. and the tantalizing aromas of fresh coffee brewing and bread toasting were drifting into the bedroom.

She felt wonderful, better than she had in over a year or even longer. There was no tightness or tension inside her, no dread of what the day might bring.

She sat up and stretched, and discovered the ache in her thighs. She was stiff, and understandably so, after the workout she had indulged in with Hawk. Standing by the bed, she noticed his clothes and shoes were gone. Well, at least she didn't have to worry about walking into the kitchen and finding him naked!

Hawk. Kate smiled at the mere thought of him. He was a fantastic lover and a gentle friend. He made her laugh and it felt so good just being with him.

So, go to him, she told herself. Enjoy being with him before he goes back to the mountains. Walking a bit stiffly, she went into the bathroom. After washing her face and brushing her teeth, she looked at her hair in the mirror. Disaster. Too hungry to care, she went back to her room, thinking that Hawk could just deal with it, messy or not.

Pulling on a different robe, one that actually was warm, she slid her feet into satin mules and headed for the kitchen. Hawk was standing at the counter, two plates, a knife, butter and a jar of marmalade in front of him, carefully removing two pieces of golden-brown bread from the toaster.

"Good morning, Hawk," Kate said quietly. "Did you sleep well?"

Turning to look at her, Hawk threw out one arm in an invitation for her to join him. "Good morning, Kate. I love your do," he said teasingly. "I slept very well, thank you," he added, curling his long arm around her shoulders when she stepped up beside him and tangling his fingers into her flyaway curls. "You?"

"Yes. Deeply. I don't even remember dreaming." She raised her brows. "Is one of those pieces for me?"

"There's a price," he said, smiling down at her.

"Hmm." She hummed as though considering his offer. "And the price is?"

"A kiss," he said at once.

"Oh, all right," she said impatiently. "But you should be darned glad I'm hungry." She raised her mouth to him, her lips parted.

Wrapping his other arm around her to draw her tightly against him, Hawk accepted her silent offer. Expecting one of his deep, ravishing kisses, Kate was pleasantly surprised by his sweet and gentle morning greeting.

"The toast is getting cold," he said, releasing her to tend to the bread.

Kate made a production of pouting.

Hawk laughed. "Don't start anything. You have to be at work in about three hours."

They laughed together and it struck Kate

that they laughed together a lot. She and the jerk had rarely laughed easily—or together.

They sat at the kitchen table and chatted about things, common things, important things, until they had finished their toast and two cups of coffee each.

Then Hawk shoved his chair back. "I'm going to get out of here to give you time to do whatever you have to do before going to work."

He pulled her into a crushing embrace and kissed her until her senses were swimming. She was breathless and thrilled when he stepped back from her to draw a deep breath.

"Do you want me to help you with the dishes?" he asked after a moment.

"You don't have to help, Hawk." She wore a suggestive smile. "But you could give me another kiss…if you don't mind."

"Mind?" He drew her back into his embrace. "I'll show you how much I mind." He took her mouth, owned it for long seconds before again releasing it, stepping back, drawing another deep breath.

"I'll see you tonight at dinner, okay?" he said in a dry croak. "Right now I'd better get outta here before I do something I'd never be sorry for." Turning, he strode from the room, her laughter following him to the door.

After setting the kitchen to rights, Kate went back into the bedroom to remove the sheets from the bed and wash them. She paused beside the bed, then began making it instead. The scent of Hawk was on her sheets, and she wanted to sleep between them again, surrounded by his masculine smell.

Kate was all but ready to go to work when the intercom buzzer sounded.

Hawk? She frowned when she realized that his name was the first thing to flash into her mind. Well, she told herself, it was understandable.

Going to the intercom, she pushed a button and said, "Yes? Who is it?"

"Florist," a young male voice answered. "I have a delivery for a Ms. Kate Muldoon."

Hmm, she thought. Hawk? Already? Suddenly she flushed with pleasure. "I'll be right down," she said into the intercom, grabbed her purse to extract several dollars for a tip, then opened the front door and ran down the steps, too eager to wait for the elevator.

A young man stood on the other side of the lobby door, smiling at her. She flipped the lock and opened the door. "Hi. Is that for me?" she said, eyeing the large cellophane-wrapped bouquet he held in one hand.

"Yep. Enjoy your flowers."

"I will," she replied handing him his tip and closing the door behind her as she stepped back with the bouquet.

Back in her apartment, Kate went into the kitchen. Setting the pale green glass vase on the countertop, she carefully removed the cellophane to reveal dark red roses.

"Oh, my," she said, unaware she had whispered aloud. The roses, her favorite flower, were just beginning to open, and each bloom looked perfect.

Suddenly realizing she had pulled the florist's card away along with the cellophane, she rummaged until she found it. Her pleasure turned to anger as she read the card.

Kate,
I am so very sorry for my obnoxious behavior last night and recently and

before, when we were together. It's just that I love you so much, the fear of losing you made me wild and I reacted badly. I know that but I beg you to please forgive me. I love you and know you love me, too. And, please don't go to a lawyer. You'd lose.

Jeff

Kate's first thought was, How did he get all that on that small card? Her second thought was, The son of a bitch.

Her anger growing into full-blown fury, she tore the card into tiny pieces, dropped them into the kitchen trash can and tossed the beautiful roses in on top of them, slamming the lid shut.

Shaking, she forced herself to take deep breaths and slowly let them out until she had calmed down. Her gaze landing on the wall clock, Kate strode from the kitchen. She had to go to work.

Hawk made an appearance mere minutes before her meal break. The sight of him as he entered the restuarant and strolled to the hostess station, where she stood, brought a sigh of sheer relief from the depths of her being. Everything would be all right now. The thought startled her. But only until he went back to Colorado, she reminded herself.

"I'm going to miss you when you're gone," she blurted. With her surprising words, an idea popped into her head. Ridiculous, she thought, mentally shaking her head. Forget it.

"Thanks, Kate." Hawk smiled back, not a bright smile but temptingly, slumberous one. "I'm going to miss you, too. You are going to join me for dinner, aren't you? I'm not heading to Colorado this second."

Still recovering from the force of his smile, Kate had to swallow before she could answer.

He picked up two menus and arched a brow. "Will you join me?"

"Yes, yes, I will." Circling around the hostess station, she led the way to a table.

"Is something wrong, Kate?" he said after he'd seated them both. "You seem far away, distracted."

"I am somewhat. I…" she began, halting when the server came to take their order. She raised her brows at Hawk. Strangely, he appeared to know what she was asking of him.

"We'll both have the special of the day," he said, glancing at her. "Wine?"

Looking up at him, she smiled. "No wine.

I'm working." She looked at the server, Gladys, a middle-aged woman with a great sense of humor. "I'll have coffee, Gladys. Before dinner, please."

"Got it," Gladys said, turning her gaze on Hawk. "What about you, Mr. McKenna?"

"Yes, ma'am," he said. "I'll have coffee, also."

Gladys was flushed with pleasure from his respectful address when she moved away from the table.

"What's the matter, Kate?" His voice held concern. Hawk paused before continuing. "Is it something I can help you with?"

Go for it, a small voice inside her said. Kate drew a deep breath, then explained every-thing that had happened.

She concluded by saying, "I tore up the card and threw it in the trash and dropped the flowers in with it. Hawk...I..." She stopped when Gladys came to the table, bearing a tray with their coffees, cream and sugar.

"Your dinners will be here shortly," Gladys informed them.

Kate added cream to her coffee, gnawing on her lip as she reconsidered her decision to share her idea with him. She was certain that if she did, he'd think she'd slipped over the edge of reason.

"Hawk…I…what?" he said, gently nudging her.

Kate opened her mouth, closed it again, swallowed, then softly and quickly asked, "Hawk, will you marry me?"

Hawk was thrown for a loop by Kate's proposal. He stared at her in dead silence for a moment. She had just finished relaying the details of the harassment and the threats that

Jeff, the jerk, had been using to frighten her. And then she tossed the proposal at him out of left field.

"Kate—" he began, but she cut him off.

"No." She was shaking her head. "I'm sorry. I don't know why…" The arrival of Gladys at their table with their dinners silenced her.

She started again the moment Gladys moved away.

"Hawk, forget what I—" she began, but he cut her off.

"No, I want to discuss this matter with you," he said, raising his hand, palm up, to keep her from talking. "Let's eat our dinner. We'll talk afterward."

Kate didn't say a word. She fidgeted. She drank her coffee in a few deep swallows. She picked at her food with a fork but ate little of it.

Watching her, Hawk silently decided that was enough. Reaching across the table, he laid his hand over hers, ending her mutilation of the fish on her plate. She glanced up at him, which had been his purpose.

"Kate." His voice was soft, gentle. "The poor fish is already dead. Calm down and eat. The food is delicious." He smiled. "You don't want to hurt Vic's feelings, do you?"

She exhaled and he could see the tension drain out of her rigid body. "Okay," she said, offering him an apologetic smile. He accepted it with one of his own before returning his attention to his meal.

Hawk cleaned off his plate, along with two rolls from the basket Gladys had set on the table with their dinners. He was pleased to note that Kate had consumed over half of her meal and part of one roll.

"Dessert?" he asked, wiping his mouth with his napkin. "More coffee?"

"Coffee. No dessert," she said, offering him a tentative smile.

He smiled back, feeling relaxed, hoping she would relax also. "Coffee it is." Before he could so much as glance around to locate Gladys, she was there, a coffee carafe in hand. She refilled the cups, collected the dinner plates and was gone again, leaving them alone.

As there were diners at the next table, Hawk kept his voice low. "Okay. What's the deal?"

"Forget it," Kate said, once again shaking her head. "It was a stupid brainstorm. That's all."

"C'mon, Kate," he said, lowering his voice even more. "We were lovers last night. You can tell me anything, even your stupid brainstorm." His smile was sweet. "I promise I won't laugh."

His efforts paid off when she returned his smile.

"Okay. Thanks, Hawk." Kate took a deep breath, as if drawing courage into herself and quickly blurted out, "I asked you to marry me to get out of Vegas for a while and away from Jeff. I'm sorry. I am at the end of my rope and scared. I didn't give a thought to the fact that I'd be using you, and that was unfair of me."

"Why not just report Jeff to the authorities?" Hawk asked reasonably.

"I did." Kate shuddered. "I should have done something when he continued to bother me after I tossed him out. I realize that now. But I was so sure he'd eventually give it up and leave me alone. I thought the restraining order would finish it." She drew a tired-sounding breath. "My mistake and now I'm paying for it."

Hawk was shaking his head. "But you talked to that lawyer yesterday. Call him or the police and tell them Jeff has threatened you."

She shook her head. "You don't understand. Jeff told me he has contacts, friends, some in court, so to speak. This is Vegas. Some of those friends might not be so friendly."

That gave him pause. His expression turned stony.

"So you decided to skip town for a while… with me?"

"No." She heaved a sigh. "The idea that stormed my brain was to ask you to marry me and remain married for a while, maybe four months or so, and to make sure Jeff hears about it. I guess I was hoping that after a time, he'd give it up and find someone else to abuse."

"Uh-huh," Hawk murmured, pondering her explanation. "And did your brainstorm come with any information for me as to how this would work?"

Kate frowned. Damned if she wasn't gorgeous, even with a scowl on her face. "Such as?" She was now staring at him through narrowed eyes.

"Hey, kid, don't look at me as though you want to strangle me." He narrowed his eyes right back at her. "You started this, you know."

Closing her eyes, Kate seemed to deflate. "Yes, I do know. I'm sorry, Hawk. Just forget it. I know I have no right to dump my troubles in your lap."

Deciding he was a damn fool, Hawk

smiled and said, "I didn't say I wouldn't do it, Kate. I just want to know what exactly you had in mind."

Eight

Kate was stunned and couldn't find her voice for a moment. "I…uh…as I said, I was thinking about a temporary arrangement, say four to six months."

Hawk's brows went up in question. "You're not suggesting we get married and stay here in Vegas for that amount of time, because if—" That was as far as he got before she cut in.

"No, of course not," she quickly said. "I know you have a ranch to run."

"That's right," he said before she could say any more. "And I'm going to have to get back soon." He only paused a second before continuing. "Look, I was thinking of leaving this weekend…."

"Oh…" she replied, disappointed.

"No, don't go jumping to any conclusions, Kate. Let me finish. Okay?"

She nodded in agreement and flicked a hand, indicating he should continue.

"Good." He smiled.

Kate felt some of the tension leak from her spine. She smiled back at him.

"First of all, though I said I was thinking about flying out this weekend, I don't have to go. I have an open-ended ticket." He paused again, this time to take a swallow of his cooling coffee. "Now, tell me what you have in mind."

"Thank you, Hawk," she said and rushed to convey the details before he could change his mind. "If you're agreeable to my proposal, I thought we could get married here in Vegas, making sure Jeff hears about it. You could then go back to Colorado immediately if you wanted to."

Hawk narrowed his eyes at her. "And you stay here in Vegas? That's not going to convince anybody."

"No, no. If you'd prefer I didn't go with you, I would find another place to stay. Maybe my father's farm in Virginia, although I'd really rather not go there."

"Why not?" he asked. "It seems reasonable to me for you to go there without the farce of a wedding."

Kate was starting to feel queasy. He wasn't going to agree to her plan, which she was starting to think was a bad one from the beginning. Smothering a sigh, she went on to explain.

"My mother died when I was in high school," she said, her voice dull. "I didn't go to college as planned but stayed home to keep house for my father. I liked the work. Cooking, cleaning, keeping the farm accounts on the computer." She paused to sip her coffee.

"You didn't resent not going to college?" Raising his coffee to his lips, Hawk watched her over the rim of his cup.

"Oh, for a while, sure, but I accepted it." She smiled. "I didn't want my father to do everything around the farm and the house by himself."

"No siblings?"

"No, at least not then. I now have two, a brother, Kent, and a sister, Erin."

Hawk smiled in understanding. "Your father remarried, and you found out you were not an exception to the rule."

Kate frowned. "What do you mean? What rule?"

"That two women can't live in harmony in the same house."

"I did try," she said defensively. "Well, maybe I didn't try hard enough." She gave him a wry smile. "I had everything the way I wanted it." She sighed. "But you know the old saying…a new broom sweeps clean."

"Hmm…" Hawk nodded. "So you took off for parts unknown. Right?"

"Yes. My father had insisted on paying me, and since I really had nothing much to spend money on, I had quite a bit saved." She shrugged. "I had a car of my own and took off to see something of the country. I landed, all but broke, here in Vegas and got lucky." She smiled. "Not in the casinos but by meeting Vic."

"And your brother and sister?" he asked, lifting a brow.

"Oh, I hung around, gritting my teeth, until after Erin was born. She's the youngest."

"You don't like kids?"

"I love kids," she said. "I just didn't want to spend years raising another woman's kids, or even helping, to tell the truth."

"Okay, so you don't want to go back to Virginia," he said. "And that brought on the idea to go back to Colorado with me?"

"Hawk, really, let's just forget it," she said, now feeling sorry for presenting the idea.

Pushing her chair back, she stood up before he could rise to help her. "Look, Hawk, I'm an idiot. Just forget I said anything. Okay?"

"No," he replied mildly. "I'm still ready to hear the rest of your plan. I'll be waiting in back tonight when you go for your car."

"But, Vic will be there," she protested.

"So?" Hawk shrugged, drawing her gaze to his wide shoulders. "I'll say hello and goodnight." He grinned. "That is, if I may follow you home."

Like the fabled phoenix, Kate's hopes rose from her ashes of defeat. "All right, Hawk. Not only may you follow me home, but you may come in for a drink."

"Now you're talkin'," he said. "You'd better get on the ball before Vic fires you."

"As if," Kate shot back at him as she hurried back to the hostess station.

Hawk left soon after. He didn't stop at the hostess station but rather touched his fingertips to his lips and blew a kiss at her. "See you later," he called, striding from the restaurant.

Kate couldn't wait. She wanted this over with. Her nerves felt like a mass of tangled live electrical wires. Fortunately, the rest of the night passed swiftly. There was only one hitch.

Close to quitting time, Kate's cell phone beeped with a text message. It was from Jeff and contained the same garbage as before: I'm sorry. Forgive me. I love you. And I know you love me. So don't do anything stupid, and call off the lawyer.

Exhaling, she lifted her hand to delete the message, then paused, deciding to keep it instead. She'd show the message to Hawk.

Maybe, just maybe it might convince him to help her.

Hawk was leaning against his rental car when she walked across the parking lot. Good heavens, he was one hunk of a man. Kate felt a chasm yawning inside her, a crevasse of longing and want. Being with him last night had been more than she had ever imagined making love with a man could be.

Love? Kate nearly staggered at the thought and came to an abrupt stop. No. She shook her head and straightened her shoulders. Love was an illusion; she had learned that the hard way. What she and Hawk had shared had been sex, great sex, but sex all the same. And in all honesty, she wanted to share it with him again.

"Hey," he called, drawing her from her musings. "Why are you just standing there?"

Pushing himself upright, he started toward her. "Are you all right?"

"Yes," she answered, getting herself moving again. "I'm fine. I…er…was thinking."

"Where's Vic? I thought he always walked you to your car." The gentleness in Hawk's eyes had been replaced by a frown.

"He's doing some paperwork. He was going to escort me out here, until I told him you would be here." Smiling, Kate unlocked and opened her car door. "I think I'll go home now," she added, sliding behind the wheel before glancing up at him. "Are you going to come?"

Hawk groaned. "Oh, lady, that is a loaded question, especially as I'm feeling loaded for bear already."

Cringing inside due to the unintentional double meaning of her question, Kate flushed with embarrassment. She felt foolish and not too bright. Not having a clue how to respond, she turned the key in the ignition, firing the engine to life, and began backing out of the space.

Laughing softly, Hawk strolled back to his car. Kate saw him squeezing his long body inside as she drove past him and into the street.

Although Kate couldn't tell if he was following her during the drive home, Hawk pulled his vehicle alongside her car just as she was stepping out of it. The devil was still smiling.

"I amuse you, do I?" she asked, swishing by him to the entrance to the building.

"Oh, Katie, you have no idea what you do to me," he said, standing close to her, whispering in her ear.

Kate's heartbeat seemed to skip and her breathing grew shallow. Inside the lobby her hand trembled, so she had trouble getting the key into the lock.

"You want me to get that for you?" Hawk's expression was somber, but amusement laced his voice.

"No, thank you," she said through gritted teeth, stabbing the key into the lock, turning the knob and striding through the lobby to the elevator.

Hawk was blessedly quiet until the elevator doors slid shut, closing them in together. "You angry at me?"

Growing warm inside, Kate shot him a glaring look. "Are you trying to make me angry?" Her attempt to sound harsh failed miserably.

The elevator jerked to a stop, the doors slid

apart and Hawk stepped out of the car, turning to hold a hand out to her. "You want to come?" he said, his lips twitching with laughter.

Ignoring his hand, head held high, Kate walked past him, saying smartly, "Grow up, McKenna."

His lips no longer twitching, Hawk roared with laughter. He laughed all the way through the living room to the kitchen, where Kate stopped, spun around and placed her hands on her hips.

"Do you want a drink or not?" she demanded, trying mightily to control her voice.

"Yes, ma'am," he replied nicely.

Kate shook her head. "You are something, Hawk," she said, her mock frown giving way to a flashing smile.

He strolled to her, shrugging off his jacket and tossing it over a chair on the way. Coming to a halt in front of her, he lifted the wrap from her shoulders, sent it flying on top of his jacket and raised her head with his hand to rub his rough thumb over her parted lips.

"You think so, huh?" he said, low and sexy. "Well, I think you're something, too. Something special."

Oh…oh…Kate's senses were going crazy. Her lips tingled from his touch, burned for the taste of his mouth on hers. Her entire body ached for his. Hawk. His name echoed through her mind. Hawk.

Closing her eyes to shield herself from the heat glowing in his, Kate gave herself a mental shake, telling herself to get it together. Before anything else, they had to talk, discuss the suggestion she was now sorry she had ever thought of, never mind mentioned to him.

"Uh…a drink," she said, her heart racing as she stepped back and turned to the refrigerator. "What would you like? Beer, wine or something stronger?"

"What are you having?" He smiled. She feared his smile was for her sudden ineptness.

"Well, as I don't often drink beer and never drink the stronger stuff, I'm having a glass of wine." *And I can't get to it soon enough,* she thought. Opening the fridge door, she withdrew a bottle of white zinfandel. "What can I get you, Hawk?"

"Do you have any red?" He was close, too close, peering over her shoulder.

"Yes, on the rack at the end of the countertop." Kate sighed with relief when he moved away from her.

They carried their wine into the living room. Kate motioned for Hawk to have a seat, while she kicked off her shoes before curling up on a corner of the couch. Her pulse rate increased when he chose to settle at the other end of it.

"Okay," he said, taking a swallow of his cabernet. "Tell me exactly what you had in mind."

Kate set her glass on the table next to the couch because her hands were shaking again. "I did, Hawk. I asked you to marry me."

One of his brows shot up. "Kate, tell me what you had in mind," he repeated concisely. "Were you thinking of a convenience marriage, one that is purely platonic?"

"Oh, no," she said at once. "I'm… I wouldn't dream of asking that of you. I had thought, as we seemed to be getting along so well, we could deal with each other for maybe four to six months."

"Live together, work together, share the same bed for half a year? Then go our separate ways, still friends, no harm done?"

Feeling her face grow warm and wanting to look away from his direct, riveting gaze, Kate held her head high, drew a steadying breath and answered, "Yes."

He was quiet for a moment, a long moment, staring into her eyes as if searching her soul. Kate held her breath.

"Okay, you've got a deal." Smiling, Hawk raised his glass to her in a silent salute.

A tremor still rippling through her body, Kate grasped the stem of her glass and returned the salute. "Thank you." Her voice was rough, barely there. She gulped a swallow of wine.

His nearly empty glass in his left hand, Hawk slid down the length of the couch to her. He held out his right hand. "Shake on it?"

Shivering, almost giddy with relief, Kate set her glass aside and placed her palm against his. His fingers curled around her hand. They shook, and then with a light tug, Hawk pulled her to him. He murmured, "A shake and a kiss. That will really seal the deal."

After reaching across her to set his glass next to hers, he drew her into his arms and captured her mouth with his own in a searing kiss.

Sealed indeed. The thought, recognizable if fuzzy, floated through Kate's mind. Or was she herself floating? She didn't care, not while Hawk was igniting a fire deep inside her with his devouring kiss.

When Hawk drew his mouth from hers, Kate found herself stretched out on the long couch, with Hawk stretched out next to her, or rather practically on top of her.

How did she get into that position when she didn't remember moving? How had Hawk managed the move without her noticing? Did it matter at all?

No. The answer was there, at the forefront of her mind. The only thing that mattered was that she was there with Hawk, secure and safe in his arms.

"That was some seal," he murmured close to her ear, stirring all kinds of delicious sensations throughout her entire body. "But maybe we should do it again…just to make sure."

He didn't give her time to answer. She didn't need time. Kate's lips were parted, ready and eager for the touch of his mouth to hers.

A second later there was a muted beep. Breaking off the kiss, Hawk raised his head to frown at her. "Was that your cell phone, or am I hearing things?"

Heaving a sigh, Kate pressed her palms against his chest. "Yes, please let me get up."

He groaned. "Can't we ignore it?" Still, he shifted, sliding from the couch to the floor.

Scrambling over him, she searched around for her purse, which she'd dropped absentmindedly when she'd come in. Finding the purse on the chair just inside the door, she dug out her cell, certain about who was calling before she looked at the display.

She was right. Softly echoing Hawk's groan, she returned to where he was lying on the floor, now with his hands behind his neck, cradling his head.

"Don't tell me," he drawled. "The sky is falling and we must run and tell the king."

Flipping to the text message she'd received earlier from Jeff, she handed the phone to him.

Hawk skimmed the text message and snorted, but before he could speak, she took the cell phone from him and flipped to the text message she'd just received, then handed the cell back again.

Before reading the new message, Hawk jackknifed to sit up. Shaking his head, he skimmed the text message. Then, tilting his head, he glanced at her and said wryly, "This clown has a one-phrase song, doesn't he?"

"Yeah," Kate answered, sighing. "He always has. Cyrano he's not. More Scarface. Now, do you see why I'm ready to skip town, so to speak?"

"Yes, but can't this lawyer you've hired take care of it?"

"Hawk, you've read those text messages. If Jeff has the powerful friends he claims to have and I feel certain he does, I really don't believe he'd spend more than a few hours in the lock-up, if that."

Hawk smiled. "Look, Katie, actually don't look so down and defeated. We've just sealed a contract of sorts. We can be in Colorado within a week."

"It will seem awful quick to everyone." She tried a smile and was pleased when it worked. Hawk was very reassuring. "I'll talk to Vic tomorrow at work. I'll explain the situation to him."

"No, you won't." His tone was flat, adamant.

Kate blinked. "Why not?"

"We're going to pull this off like the real thing," he said in the same tone as before. "You know, love at first sight, head over heels, the whole razzle-dazzle. We do have this physical attraction going for us. I'm sure we can appear the picture of not-so-young love."

"I beg your pardon," Kate said indignantly. "Speak for yourself when it comes to age, mister."

Hawk grinned. "You know what I mean, woman. Neither one of us will see our early twenties again. Hell, I won't see my early thirties again."

Suddenly relaxed and easy with him, Kate nodded. "I suppose you're right. That would be the best way to go about it. While I do want the news of our marriage to get back to Jeff, and it will, the chances of the truth getting to him as well are too high even if I tell only Vic."

"I know." Hawk nodded. "Vic would tell Lisa, and who knows where the information would go from there."

"You're right," Kate agreed. "I certainly wouldn't want Jeff showing up at your place."

"Ahh…Katie, you won't have to worry about that. I'm certainly not afraid of him. Besides, I'm a crack shot with a pistol or rifle. I have a foreman and a wrangler who are almost as good with a weapon as I am. Added to that, I have a dog, a very big dog that can bring down a wolf…or a man if necessary."

Kate stared at him warily, not sure if he was putting her on or not. "You wouldn't…" She didn't finish; she didn't have to. Somehow she knew he would if necessary.

"Shoot a man?" he asked. "I did, while I

was in the air force. I didn't like it. It was him or me. Sucker lived."

Kate could accept that answer. She nodded. "Okay, we do it your way. I'll simply say it didn't work out when in four or six months I return to Vegas…if I decide to return to Vegas." Before she could as much as raise a hand, she yawned.

"The mood's gone, isn't it?" Hawk looked and sounded disappointed, but his smile held understanding.

"I'm afraid so," Kate admitted. "I'm very tired. Stress, I suppose."

"I can imagine, being bugged and frightened by that SOB." He got to his feet. "Okay, I'm leaving now. I'll meet you at the restaurant tomorrow. We should be together and have our act together when we talk to Vic. That work for you, Kate?"

"Yes, Hawk, that works for me."

He went to the door, Kate behind him. At the door he turned to gaze into her eyes.

"One kiss?" he asked.

Her answer came with the lift of her head. His kiss was warm and gentle and comforting.

"Sleep well, Kate."

"You, too, Hawk."

Right, Hawk thought. He'd be lucky if he slept at all. What had he just committed himself to? Marriage? Sure, he had thought maybe someday, with the right woman. But he had never met that right woman.

Pulling into the line of cars at the valet service at his hotel, Hawk unfolded himself from the car, handed his keys to the valet, accepted his receipt and strolled into the casino.

Since he was positive he wasn't going to sleep well, Hawk decided to pass some time playing poker. Within less than an hour, and with the loss of a couple hundred-dollar bills, he pushed away from the table and went to his room.

Standing sleepless once more at the floor-to-ceiling window overlooking the busy Strip, Hawk sipped the beer he had removed from the small in-room bar, contemplating his future, at least the next four to six months of it.

Starting tomorrow afternoon he had to play a man madly in love with Kate Muldoon. He smiled. Well, it shouldn't be too onerous. Kate was a lovely woman, easy to be with, a comfortable companion and fantastic to be with in bed. In truth, she was a wonderful woman to make love with.

Love.

Was it possible for a man used to being on his own for the most part ever to find real love…if there was such a thing? And, if he should find that woman, would she be willing to spend the major part of her life stuck with him in the lee of mountains located in the back of beyond?

Hawk sighed, wondering if Kate, never mind any other woman, would even last as long as four months.

Hawk was, at that point in time, firmly stuck between anticipation and a strange sensation of something he couldn't put a name to.

A wry smile shadowed his mouth. If nothing else, Kate being at the ranch should discourage Brenda, the daughter of Hawk's foreman, Jack, from her intentions, whatever they were, in regard to him.

Nine

Fortunately Hawk had warned Kate that the ride would be bumpy after they left the macadam road. His truck was a big work-horse, and it had been comfortable up until he turned onto the private dirt road.

"Almost home now," he said, smiling at her while keeping his eyes on the excuse for a road. "Are you okay?" Obviously he had noticed her death grip on the handle mounted above the door window.

"I'm fine," Kate answered. "Or I will be as soon as we're there and I can move around again."

"Won't be long now." He hazarded a quick glance at her. "I imagine you're tired."

"A little," she said wryly. "It's been a pretty hectic day."

He laughed. "It's been a hectic week."

"Yes." A tire hit a pothole, and Kate's butt lifted from the seat for an instant, landing with a painful jar to her spine.

To her mind, they couldn't get off this miserable road fast enough. But, all things considered, the past week had gone by smoothly and swiftly.

The day after Hawk had agreed to her marriage idea, he had shown up at the restaurant moments after she had arrived for work. Together they had sought out Vic. They both knew he had to be convinced that they had almost immediately fallen in love, which wouldn't be a snap, as Vic was a very shrewd man.

The performance began with Hawk asking Vic if they could talk in private. Readily agreeing, though eyeing both of them with a curiosity bordering on suspicion, Vic led them into his small office.

"What's up?" he asked, getting directly to the point.

Encircling her waist with his arm, Hawk took over. "I'm stealing your hostess away, Vic."

Vic looked from one to the other, his suspicions now completely awakened. "What exactly do you mean by stealing Kate?" His gaze settled on her. "You want the day off to spend with the warrior here?" He indicated Hawk with a jerk of his head.

Pulling her closer to him, Hawk answered for her. "No, Vic, she doesn't want the day off to spend with me. Kate's going to leave to spend the rest of her life with me at the ranch."

"What the hell?" Vic exclaimed, his expression a mixture of shock and disbelief. "What are you talking about, Hawk? Is this some kind of a joke?"

"You know me better than that, Vic," Hawk answered. "I wouldn't joke about something this serious. I love Kate, I'm going to marry her as soon as possible and I would like you to be my best man."

His expression now oscillating between delight and confusion, Vic stared at Kate. "Is he serious? No, I can tell he's serious. What about you, Kate?"

"I'm very serious, Vic," she said, her voice soft but rock steady. "I love him." Kate turned to gaze up at Hawk in what she hoped was close to adoration. In truth, it wasn't difficult....

She had no time to contemplate the questions rising to nag at her mind. Without further probing, Vic let out a whoop and snatched Kate from Hawk to give her a big brotherly hug.

"Of course I'll be your best man, chump," he told Hawk. "Hell, I always was the best man."

"Not in this lifetime or any other," Hawk retorted, extending his right hand to Vic. "We want to get married as quickly as possible." He pulled Kate gently from Vic and back into his arms. "Don't we, Katie?"

"Yes, we do," she whispered, lowering her eyes and easily managing a soft sigh.

IN THE ARMS OF THE RANCHER

Vic was grinning and rubbing his hands together. Kate thought she could almost see the wheels rolling inside his head. "Okay, I have an idea."

Kate smiled. Vic always had an idea and was usually dead right with it.

"Go on," she said.

"I was sure you would," Hawk drawled.

Vic looked at Kate. "Were you thinking of getting married in one of the hotels or chapels?"

"Lord no," Kate yelped.

Vic smiled happily. "I was hoping you'd say that. Now, would you like to be married right here, in the restaurant, with the customers as witnesses?"

"Yes!" Kate and Hawk declared in unison.

"Then go do what you have to do," Vic said, flicking a hand to send them away. "I'll take care of everything."

"But…" Kate protested, "don't you need me at the hostess station?"

"We'll manage." Vic hugged her again. "Go. Be together. I have things to do, people to talk to, the first one being Lisa."

"Oh, that reminds me," Kate said. "I must call Lisa to ask her to be my matron of honor."

"I'll take care of that, too." Vic grinned. "She is going to be so excited. I can't wait to tell her. So, kids, get lost. Come back for supper."

Kate and Hawk went shopping, though not together. She went shopping for a special dress. He, she found out later, went shopping for wedding bands…plural. Kate couldn't have been more surprised days later, when after Hawk placed a gold band on her finger, Vic handed her a matching band to slide onto Hawk's finger.

It was a beautiful wedding. After sending Bella shopping for decorations, Vic had drafted all the employees, and any of the customers who wanted to help, to festoon the restaurant with yards of white tulle and dozens of white silk flowers. Everyone had enjoyed every minute of the fun, and when they had finished, the decorations had looked so good, Vic had decided to keep them up permanently.

Kate smiled in remembrance of the serious, fun but long wedding day. She and Hawk had left the party, still in full swing, just in time to catch the flight to Colorado that he had booked them on.

Now, tired to exhaustion, Kate was relieved when Hawk steered the truck onto a smoother surface before coming to a stop in front of a large ranch house with a deep porch that ran the entire width.

Pulling the hand brake, Hawk heaved a deep sigh and turned to smile at her. "I'm dragging, Kate. What about you?"

"I feel the same," she said, sighing as deeply as he had. "Why are there lights on in the house?" she asked, frowning. "I hope you don't have company, because I'm light years away from entertaining tonight."

"I only rarely get company, Kate, and never without forewarning." Pushing his truck door open, he jumped to the ground. "I contacted my foreman to ask him to turn on the lights for us."

"Oh, okay." She turned to open her door only to find him coming to a halt beside it. He offered his hand to help her out, and she gratefully accepted, knowing full well there was no way she'd jump out the way he had. She'd be happy if she could walk straight after the long and bumpy ride from the small airport.

Kate didn't need to walk. Hawk swept her up into his arms, drew her from the truck and carried her up the porch steps. He paused to turn the doorknob and nudge the door open with one foot before carrying her into the house, which would be her home for the next four to six months.

"You left the truck door open," she said after he set her feet firmly on the floor.

"Yeah, I know." Hawk smiled. "Welcome home, Kate. And make yourself at home. Walk around to get the stiffness out of your muscles. Explore the place while I get our bags from the truck."

Kate was happy to move about; she even did a few quick stretching exercises before exploring. She was standing in a large, comfortably decorated living room, her attention riveted on a beautiful Indian woven rug, which took up most of one wall. The living room flowed into a smaller room, the dining room, which opened to a large eat-in kitchen. A hallway ran from the living room to what she surmised were the bed- and bathrooms. She fell in love with the place at first sight.

Kate was still standing there admiring the woven rug on the wall when Hawk entered, lugging their bags.

"What do you think so far?" Hawk raised his eyebrows and dropped their luggage to the floor with a thud.

"I like it." Kate smiled a bit nervously. "Very much what I've seen of it so far."

"Good." He didn't return her smile as he

studied her expression. "You're nervous, right?"

Kate nodded. "A little, yes."

He moved to her side and lifted her head as he lowered his to brush his lips over hers. "There's no need to be, Kate," he said. "There's no rush about anything, and that includes sleeping arrangements. Anything you want or need, just say it. I'll do my best to provide."

As the nervous anxiety she'd been caught up in drained from her, Kate smiled and rattled off her present wants and needs.

"Let's see," she began, smiling up at him. "I want and need a shower, a change of clothes, food, a glass of wine and ten hours of sleep, not necessarily in that order. Actually, I believe I'd like the food and wine first. No wait, I need a bathroom first."

Hawk was laughing as he waved a hand at the hallway. "The first bedroom on the right," he said after catching his breath. "It's mine and I have my own bathroom. I'll pour the wine and rummage in the fridge to see what's available. Take your time."

"Thank you." Before heading for the hallway, Kate scooped up her carry-on bag from where he had dropped it. She entered the first door on the right.

Hawk's bedroom was spacious, big enough to hold a tallboy chest of drawers, a double dresser, a wall of sliding closet doors, a man's club chair and, in the middle of it all, a king-size bed. She stared at the bed, which was covered by a puffy comforter, for several long seconds until necessity made her turn away.

Intending only to avail herself of the facilities and wash her hands and face, Kate looked longingly at the shower for a few moments.

Oh, she could hardly wait. But first, carefully lifting from her suitcase the gorgeous off-white dress she had found in one of the upscale shops in Hawk's hotel, she shook it out and neatly draped it over the back of the club chair. Quickly stripping off her jeans, sweater and underwear, she stepped into the shower. She gave a long sigh of pure pleasure as the water flowed over her tired body. Oh, it was sheer heaven.

Kate could have stood under the spray forever if it hadn't been for the water beginning to run cold and for the fact that Hawk was waiting for her.

After drying off and quickly blow-drying her hair so that it was only slightly damp, Kate pulled out the panties, nightgown and lightweight, thigh-length robe she always packed in her carry-on bag. Digging out a brush, she smoothed her riot of curls the best she could. As she left the bedroom, she decided she owed it to Hawk to sleep there that night and every night, and she realized that she wanted to, as well. Kate quietly walked barefoot to the kitchen.

Although she didn't know how Hawk heard her enter, he must have, because he turned, raising that one brow as he gave her robed figure and still damp hair the once-over.

"I couldn't resist your shower," she explained. "I felt kind of yucky."

"Yucky, huh?" He smiled, warming her from the outside in. "You smell good…like soap or shampoo."

Kate returned the smile. "Both, I think." She inhaled. "Something else smells good."

"It's what my father always calls comfort food. I'm heating soup and making grilled cheese sandwiches."

"Tomato soup," she said, inhaling again. "The best comfort food."

He shot a quick grin at her. "It's about ready. Have a seat."

Kate was about to ask him if there wasn't something she could do to help when she glanced at the table and found that it was set for two, with wine in stemmed glasses and water in sturdy, heavier glasses.

"It looks like you're pretty handy in the kitchen," she observed, seating herself at the table.

"I've been here alone, except for the occasional guest or two, for almost ten years." Carrying two soup bowls, he crossed to the table and set one in front of her and the other at the place setting opposite.

"Ten years," she repeated, surprised.

"I quickly learned to cook and take care of myself."

He smiled, turning to the countertop to pick up two luncheon plates. "I've got a shelf full of cookbooks and I use them, too."

"Books…books, damn," Kate said, grimacing. "I packed up all my books to go with the things I put into storage." She glanced at Hawk, to find him watching her in apparent bemusement. "Like Jefferson said, 'I cannot live without books.'" She quoted the author of the Declaration of Independence. "And I'd wager the closest bookstore is in Durango. Right?"

"Most likely. I've never checked," he drawled. "But don't fret, Katie. There's always Amazon. Besides, I've got a bookcase jammed with both fiction and nonfiction hardcover keepers." He smiled. "You can spend the winter curled up with a book, warm and safe from the elements."

"Not on your life." Kate gave him an indignant look. "I never intended to have a vacation here. I haven't the temperament or the patience to lounge around all day while other people work." She paused for a breath, noticing Hawk appeared mildly taken aback by her outburst.

Kate lowered her voice. "I'm sorry," she apologized. "But I want to help out with whatever I can. Be useful, you know? Don't forget, I was raised on a working farm."

His lips twitching, Hawk held up his hands in surrender. "Okay, if that's what you want, I'll put you to work." The twitch gave way to a smile. "So, now, do you want to negotiate salary?"

Kate's head snapped up, chin thrust out; her spine stiffened. "Are you looking for a fight?"

Leaning back in his chair, Hawk erupted with laughter. When he could breathe again, he teased, "Ahh, Kate Muldoon McKenna, you are a fiery one, aren't you?"

Kate flushed and smiled at the same time. Hearing him call her McKenna sent a tingling chill through her. After the past crazy days reality finally hit her. This wasn't a dream or make-believe. She was Hawk McKenna's legal wife, if only on a temporary basis. *His*. In a weird way, after knowing him not even two full weeks, Kate kind of liked the idea.

The ghost of his smile still played over his mouth. "What's going on in that busy mind of yours?"

Kate returned his smile. "I was just thinking

how strange it sounded to hear you call me Kate McKenna," she said.

"You'll get used to it." He chuckled. "What you'll hear after I've introduced you to my men is Ms. McKenna whenever they address you."

"How long will that last?" she asked, frowning. "I'd much rather they call me Kate."

"Oh, they will in time." He grinned. "They'll have to get used to you first. Take your measure."

"In other words, they're going to be judging me." Kate wasn't sure she liked that idea.

His lips quivered. "Sure, they'll want to make sure you're good enough for me."

"Good enough!" Kate said, anger sparking until she saw him silently laughing at her. "You are a devil, aren't you? Well, I'll show you and your men how good enough I am."

"I already know," he reminded her. "As for my men, go to it…after we've taken a few days for, as my foreman called it, honeymooning."

Kate rolled her eyes.

Hawk laughed.

Together, they cleared away the supper dishes, all but the wineglasses. When the kitchen had been set to rights, he asked, "As you already had your shower, food and wine, are you now ready for sleep?"

"The shower, food, wine and conversation gave me my second wind. I'm not nearly as sleepy as before." She held her glass out to him. "I'd like to have a little more wine, crawl into bed, prop myself up against some pillows and relax while I finish my drink."

Hawk half filled both glasses before saying, "There are two other bedrooms and a central bath on the left side of the hall, opposite my bedroom. Have you decided where you're going to sleep?"

She gave him what she hoped was a sexy, come-hither smile. "My toiletries bag is in your bathroom."

He sent a smile back at her that heated her blood as it tap-danced up her spine. She reached for her glass. He held it aloft.

"Lead on, Kate. I'm right behind you."

She set off for the hallway.

He followed her. "And, since the word *behind* is out there, you have a very enticing one."

In retaliation, Kate wiggled her hips. With a low wolf whistle, he followed her into his bedroom.

Hawk plumped the pillows for her, waited while she crawled into the bed then handed the glass of wine to her. "Comfortable?" he asked.

"Very," she replied, snuggling against the pillows. She felt almost lost in the wide expanse of bed. "Oh, Hawk, this is heaven."

"Not yet, but I have hopes," he said, his gaze seeming to touch her in very delicate spots.

Kate drew a quick breath. "Oh, my." She took a quick sip of the cold wine in hopes of dousing the heat shimmering through her.

"My sentiments exactly." Inhaling, he turned away, setting his glass on the dresser. "I'm going to have a shower. I won't be long."

Reclining against the pillows, too warm all over, Kate kicked the comforter and top sheet to the bottom of the bed. Raising her left hand to take another sip of wine, her gaze caught on the gold band circling her third finger. Unlike Hawk's plain gold ring, the band he had chosen for her was covered with pavé diamonds.

It was beautiful and felt oddly right on her finger, as if it belonged there. Taking more swallows of wine, she continued to gaze at the ring, contemplating the intrinsic, sacred meaning behind the exchange of marriage bands.

Dear Lord, what had she done?

Catching her lower lip between her teeth, her gaze locked on the ring, she felt the sting of incipient tears in her eyes. In her determination to get away from one man, a nasty, possibly dangerous man, she had talked a good man, a decent, wonderful man, into a loveless marriage. It was terribly unfair of her. He deserved better.

The tears overflowed her lower lids just as Hawk, a towel wrapped around his hips, came into the room. He stopped short by the side of the bed.

"Tears," he said, his voice and expression concerned. "Are you feeling regrets?"

"No… Yes, but it's not what you think," she said, sniffing.

Without a word, he walked to the dresser, opened a small side drawer and withdrew a man's snowy-white handkerchief and a foil-wrapped packet. Moving around to the side of the bed she was lying on, he handed the hankie to her and laid the packet on the night-stand.

"Now, what is this 'no…yes'? It's not what I think it is?" Holding the towel with one hand, he took the glass from her trembling hand and set it on the nightstand, next to the foil packet.

Blinking to disperse the tears, which didn't work, she sniffed again and brought the hankie to her nose. "I…I'm sorry. I had no right."

Holding on to the slipping towel, Hawk carefully sat on the edge of the bed, next to her. "If I heard correctly, you mumbled that you had no right." Taking the hankie from her hands, he mopped away the tears. "No right to what?"

Kate sniffed twice, drew a couple deep breaths and shakily answered, "I had no right to talk you into this farce." She sniffed once more. "I'm sorry."

"Kate." Hawk's voice was soft, soothing. "You didn't talk me into anything. If I hadn't wanted to do it, you could have talked your head off, and I'd have said, 'No, thank you, but no.'"

"Oh…" She blinked again.

"Right. Oh." He smiled. "Now, in case you haven't noticed, I'm shivering here. That's because I'm cold. Move over and share the warmth."

Kate shimmied over to let him in.

His gaze skimmed the top of the bed, from her head to her waist. "Where's the sheet and comforter?"

"I was already warm, so I shoved them to the bottom," she admitted. "I'll get them."

"Stay put," he said, turning to grab the covers with his free hand and pull them up and over most of her. "Do you want your wine?"

"No, I'm finished for tonight." Kate quickly lowered her eyes as he lifted his rear off the bed to yank off the towel and toss it to the floor.

"I've had enough, too," he said, sliding into the bed, next to her. "Why are you looking away, Kate? You've seen me naked before."

"Yes, I know," she said, her voice barely a whisper. "But that was before we were married."

Silence. Dead silence. Kate was getting jittery. All of a sudden laughter rumbled in his chest before roaring from his throat.

"Kate, oh, Kate, you are a joy to be with." Rolling to and over her, he cradled her face with his big hands and kissed the nervousness out of her.

She didn't respond, well not verbally. But she kissed him back as if her very sanity depended on his kiss. Then again, maybe it did.

Their lovemaking was even more intense, more exhilarating than before. This time Kate and Hawk reached the summit together.

Completely exhausted, refusing to get out of his bed for any reason, she curled her arm around his waist when he returned from the bathroom, rested her cheek on his still moist chest and closed her eyes.

Hawk slid his fingers into her loose curls, holding her to him. "Good night, Kate." He kissed her hair.

Kate sighed with contentment. "Good night, Hawk." Closing her eyes, she immediately began to drift.

The marriage was consummated. It was her last thought before drifting into a deep sleep.

Ten

Hawk had set aside four whole days for them to honeymoon. They didn't spend the entire four days in bed, or even three days. But they did spend three of those days in the house, hanging out, reading, eating, having sex, unbelievable, breathtaking sex.

The fourth day they went outside. Unlike the mild, warm October days in Vegas, in the mountains there was a definite chill in the air in the afternoon and the nights were cold, a harbinger of approaching winter.

Hawk had mentioned showing her his horses, at least some of them. She had no idea he had so very many. Kate supposed she should have realized this, as Vic had told her that Hawk bred beautiful horses.

It was a glorious autumn day. There was a nip in the air, but the sunshine was brilliant in a gorgeous deep blue sky. The leaves on the mountain's deciduous trees had begun to fall but the sight was still spectacular.

Caught up in the beauty of this valley nestled in the mountain range, Kate was startled when Hawk, curling his hand around hers, broke her reverie.

"We're having company, Kate," he said, turning her a half step.

In the near distance Kate saw two men riding toward them. "Your men?"

"Yeah," he answered, raising a hand in a welcoming wave. "Coming to meet the Mrs., so please stay in wife mode."

"Well, of course," she said, both hurt and mad, glaring up at him. She could have saved herself the display of annoyance, because beneath the wide brim of the Western hat he had settled on his head before leaving the house, his gaze was fixed on the riders. She now knew the reason he had at times reach to touch a brim that wasn't there while he was in Vegas.

Before he had donned his hat, Hawk had plopped one on her head. Now she was glad he had, as the wide brim shaded her eyes from the dazzling sunlight.

The two riders slowed to a walk as they drew near her and Hawk and pulled up a couple of feet in front of them. Jumping down from his mount, a middle-aged man of medium height and with a sturdy body strolled over to Hawk, his hand outstretched.

"Mornin', Hawk. Ted and I came to meet the wife. I hope we're not intruding."

Hawk gave them a droll look. "Figured," he drawled, turning to her. "Kate, I want you to meet my foreman, Jack, right here, and Ted, the fellow next to Jack, is the best wrangler in the state."

She smiled and nodded at both men. "Jack, Ted, I'm pleased to meet you both." She noticed that Ted was younger than Jack, taller and as slim as a whip.

"Nice to meet you, ma'am," the men said in unison. "We were wonderin' when the boss here was goin' to find a good woman to keep 'im in line," Jack added.

Kate laughed. "Needs to be kept on a short leash, does he?" she said, grinning up at Hawk.

"Yessum, Ms. McKenna," Ted chimed in. "The boss here has a tendency to work too hard."

"That's right," Jack confirmed. "Forgets there's more to livin' than babyin' horses."

Kate laughed, already liking the men.

"Okay, you two, knock off the comedy and get back to work." Hawk interjected. "I'll be with you in a little while."

Both men chuckled, then remounted and rode off in the direction of a pasture with a good number of horses moving around in it. Jack called back, "Take your time, Hawk, if you have better things to do."

Hawk shook his head. Kate smiled. "I like

your men, Hawk," she said. "They seem very nice."

"They are good men," he said. "You'll be seeing them again this Saturday. We've invited them to a reception, of sorts."

Kate shot a startled look at him, but he continued speaking.

"Ted and his wife, Carol, and Jack and his daughter, Brenda, will be here Saturday evening, after we've packed it in for the day. Jack's been divorced for close to seven years now. Brenda has spent most of her summers here, at least five, during those years. Carol's a lovely woman. She and Ted have been married two years." He arched that same brow again. "Okay?"

"Okay what?" she asked. "Okay that we have a reception or okay that Ted and Carol have been married two years?" Somehow she managed to keep a straight face.

Now he shook his head in despair at her. "Can you ride?"

"Yes, I can." She put on a haughty expression. "Rather well, too. But first I have a question."

"Shoot," he said.

"Do you…we…have the makings for a party on Saturday night?"

"Plenty of stuff in the pantry and freezer," he answered. "And plenty of beer, wine and soft drinks. Do you have any favorite foods?"

"I'll give it some thought." She smiled. "Now I'm ready for a ride."

"Good." Taking her hand, he led her to the stables. "Let's saddle up, and I'll give you a short tour of the place before I get to work with the men."

Walking by Hawk's side to the stables, Kate was struck by the sudden realization of how completely different her life and lifestyle had been since leaving Vegas. Where she used to sleep in because of working the late hours, now she was up before dawn to prepare Hawk's breakfast. At first, she wasn't too happy about it, but now she enjoyed cooking for him, watching him dig in to the food she had made.

Hawk needed to spend time on ranch chores despite the honeymoon, and he always showered before dinner. He came to the table smelling of shaving cream and pure male. Before the first week was over, Kate was showering with him while the evening meal simmered.

"So, what do you think?"

The sound of his voice drew her from bemusement and Kate glanced up to look at the horse he was saddling. He had picked out a gentle roan mare for her and told her Ted had named the mare Babycakes. Kate was happy with his choice and the name. She was surprised when she saw the horse he saddled for himself. It was the biggest horse she had ever seen, other than draft horses.

As they trotted side by side to the pasture, one of several she later learned, she felt like a child on a pony next to Hawk on the tall, sleek animal.

As they circled around, both she and Hawk waved to Jack and Ted as they worked the horses, before heading on to the pasture beyond.

With the sunlight playing on their sleek coats, the horses looked beautiful, well kept and cared for. "Have you always been a horse man?"

Hawk smiled. "Yes, I fell in love when my father bought me my first horse, a filly." He slanted his head, his smile morphing into a grin. "And here comes my second animal love." Pulling up his mount, he jumped down and turned just as a large animal streaked by Kate's horse and leapt straight at Hawk.

"Hawk, watch out…" Kate cried just as the animal made the jump. Fear caught her breath. Gulping in air, she couldn't believe her eyes or ears.

Hawk was on the ground, laughing. She could now see that the animal on top of him was a very big dog. The dog's tail was swishing back and forth a mile a minute, its tongue lapping every inch of Hawk's face.

"Yeah, Boyo, I love you, too, but get off me now. You're crushing my ribs."

To Kate's surprise, the dog immediately jumped to the side, as if he understood every word. Hawk ruffled the dog's wiry-looking coat before getting to his feet. Walking to the side of her horse, he grinned up at her.

"Boyo?" was all she said.

He laughed. "Yep, Boyo. It's Irish slang for *boy*." The dog came to stand next to him. Hawk placed his hand on the dog's large head. "This is the Irish wolfhound I told you about."

Kate gave the dog a dubious glance. "Does he resent competition?"

Hawk caught on at once and grinned at her. "No, or at any rate, he tolerates it, and that includes every person on the property."

The sigh Kate exhaled wasn't all show. "That's a relief. He's kind of frightening."

"Nah," Hawk said, shaking his head. "He's a pushover for anyone willing to scratch his head."

"I'll keep that in mind," she said.

Nevertheless, she made sure she didn't ride too close to Boyo on the way back to the stable. This time Kate noticed a large white circle between the stable corral and the pasture.

She looked at Hawk. "Is that a helipad over there?"

"Yes, I put it in for rescue purposes, in case of an emergency with either the people or the animals."

"Do you own the chopper?" she asked as she dismounted.

"No, I use a rescue service," he explained as he jumped off his horse. "But I could fly a chopper. I flew a Black Hawk in the service, and I practice now and again."

"Cool," she quipped, giving him a high five.

Kate learned that her wariness of the dog was unnecessary once they were in the house. Boyo nudged her leg with his long snout twice until she hesitantly lowered her hand to his head to give him a brisk scratch. He was immediately her best friend. Kate fell in love with the big, ferocious-looking baby.

Kate spent the next few days getting ready for the reception. While Hawk was outside working with his men, she prepared numerous dishes. Some she had found in his cookbooks; others she had learned from her mother.

She was nervous Saturday evening, before their guests arrived. Hawk came into the house and brushed his mouth over hers on his way to the bathroom for a shower. As he swept by, she caught a whiff of fresh air, horse, sweaty male and Hawk's personal scent. For a moment, she was tempted to join him in the shower.

Kate gave a heartfelt sigh. Living with Hawk was so good…but it was not permanent. The physical life they shared in bed almost every night was wonderful. His sudden quick kisses made her head spin. She knew she wasn't falling in love with him, because she was fathoms deep already.

She knew Hawk loved kissing her, making love with her, but she also knew he was skeptical about the very word *love*. He simply didn't believe in romantic love, the forever after kind. She wished…

The realization of time passing sent her back into the kitchen. Hawk was beside her in record time. "How's it going? Can I do anything to help?"

"Fine and no," she answered, stirring the mouthwatering, aromatic beef barbecue, one of her mother's recipes.

"Lordy, that smells good, and I'm starving." He caught her chin in his hand to turn her to face him. "Hungry, too," he murmured, kissing her senseless.

Kate shoved him away after a few heavenly minutes. "I've got to get this together," she said, grabbing a breath between each word. "Pitch in, lover."

Hawk gave a fake shudder. "Oh, Katie, hearing you call me lover turns me on."

"Later," she said, flashing a smile at him. "Right now I do believe our guests have arrived."

"I'm going to hold you to that," he said, moving away from her.

"I certainly hope so," she replied, laughing as he tossed a wicked grin back at her.

The reception was wonderful. Everyone chattered, laughed and even sang. Kate liked Carol at once. She was young but mature with a great sense of humor.

After Carol, Hawk led Kate over to Jack to introduce her to his daughter. Brenda was a pretty girl, in her late teens, Kate judged.

With a murmured "excuse me, ladies," Jack wandered to where the men were gathered, Hawk handing out cans of beer.

"I'm glad to meet you, Brenda," Kate said, extending her hand to the girl.

"Likewise," the girl replied, a sweet, miss-innocent smile on her face as she took Kate's hand in a crushing grip.

Managing to keep from wincing in pain, Kate tightened her own fingers harder around the girl's hand.

Glaring at her, Brenda gave in, withdrawing her hand.

Despite the tingle of pain in her fingers, Kate met Brenda's glare with a serene smile. "Now, if you will excuse me, I have to check on the food cooking on the stove."

Oh, boy, Kate thought, making her way to the kitchen. In her estimation, Brenda was walking, talking, snotty trouble. There was something sly and petulant about her that sounded an alarm inside Kate's mind. But why had the girl targeted her? Hawk's soft laughter came from across the room.

Of course. Kate sighed. Brenda was infatuated with Hawk. Kate couldn't blame Brenda. Hawk was all the things of many women's dreams, but he was way out of the young girl's league.

A sense of foreboding rippled through

Kate, a warning of unpleasant things, scenes to come.

The festivities lasted long into the night. Finally, but reluctantly, the party broke up. Kate stood next to Hawk on the porch, grateful for his arm around her to ward off the night cold, still talking to the others as they made their way to their vehicles.

"You throw one hell of a party, lady," Hawk said, praising her efforts once everyone had left. "Thanks."

"You're welcome, and thank you for the compliment, sir." Standing on tiptoes, she kissed him on the side of his sculpted, hard jaw. "Now you may help me clear the mess away inside."

"Aw, gee, Kate," he groused like a kid. "Can't we leave it till morning? I gotta work, ya know?"

But Hawk pitched in right beside her, heaving deep, put-upon sighs every few minutes. By the time they were finished, Kate was laughing. She wasn't laughing a short time later, after they were in bed. She was crying out in delicious pleasure.

Kate had dinner ready for him when he came in to eat as the sun went down the next day. While he dug into his food like a starving man, they did a postmortem of the reception the night before.

"I like your friends," she said, handing the dish of mashed potatoes to him for a second helping. "And I could tell at once that they are friends as well as employees."

Nodding, Hawk swallowed before replying. "They are," he said. "Good thing, too, especially during the winter months. We get together often...." He smiled and took another roll from the bread basket. "If we didn't, we'd likely all get antsy with cabin fever."

Kate laughed and gave him an arch look. "And here, all this time I was thinking you were a loner."

"I don't mind being alone," he said, picking up his coffee cup. "Fact is there are times I prefer it."

"Like when you want to read?"

"Yes, and when I'm watching football."

"Uh-huh." Kate tilted her head, fighting a smile. "Is this your way of reminding me there's a game on tonight and you don't want to be bothered?"

"No, because you don't bother me." Standing, he took both their plates, carried them to the sink and came back to the table with the coffee carafe. "Do you like football?"

"I can tolerate it," she admitted. "But I'd rather read."

He was pensive a moment. "I could go into the bedroom to watch the game on the set in there," he offered, pleasing her with his thoughtfulness.

Kate was shaking her head before he'd finished. "That's not necessary. If I'm into a story, I don't even hear the TV unless it's blaring."

"It won't be." Hawk slanted a slow smile at her. "I could watch the game in the living room and you could read your book in bed," he suggested.

Kate laughed. "No, you may watch in the game in bed. I can't get comfortable reading in bed."

He heaved a sigh. "Will you sit next to me and read if I watch the game while sitting on the sofa?"

"I will if you'll refill my cup," she said, reminding him he was still standing there with the carafe in hand. "Can we get back to our discussion about the reception now that our seating arrangement for tonight has been confirmed?" She grinned.

He grinned back, causing a melting sensation inside her. "Sure we can." He frowned. "Something about it on your mind?"

"Well…it's about Brenda."

Hawk groaned. "What about her? Was she rude to you? Did she insult you in some way?"

"Not exactly." Kate paused, searching for the right words. "I tried to draw her into a conversation. She seemed so, oh, I don't know, almost sullen." She sighed. "She wasn't very responsive."

He drew a deep breath. "I was going to talk to you about Brenda. I should have done it before the party. She is, and has been for some time, a pain in the neck and parts south." He ran his fingers through his long hair, loosening it from the leather thong.

Kate smiled at his ruffled strands of hair. His expression serious, Hawk untied the thong and shook his head, freeing the long locks.

"As I was saying," he went on, ignoring her obvious urge to laugh, "Brenda has been coming to the ranch for a long time. When she was younger, she was a high-spirited kid. Jack and I taught her to ride." He grimaced. "When she arrived here after graduating from high school, a year ago this coming summer, she was different."

"In what way?"

"Kate, the only way to describe it is that she began hanging around me too much." He shook his head. "Understand she had always hung around, but that summer it was different. At first I thought she was just using me to practice her wiles to use on younger men. But it wasn't that. She started *accidentally* brushing against me…with her breasts, touching me, hugging me." His smile was wry. "I'm not stupid. Her actions were not the same as when she was a young girl. She was coming on to me. I did talk to Jack about it before I left for Vegas, and he assured me he'd take care of it. Looks like his lecture went in one ear and out the other."

"And now," Kate said, "I suspect Brenda, the temptress in training, resents the woman you brought home with you from Las Vegas."

Sighing again, Hawk finished his coffee and began to clear the table. Kate got up to help him. "That's the way I figure it," he said. "I suppose I'll have to talk to her, tell her a few home truths."

"Ahh, no, Hawk, I'll talk to her, at the right moment." She knew her smile wasn't sweet. "I'll be gentle, but firm."

The right moment appeared the following week. Kate was on the phone. She had received a call from her father, the fourth since Kate had told him she had married Hawk and moved with him to his ranch in Colorado. She was actually gushing in an attempt to finally convince him she was safe, well and over-the-moon happy.

No sooner had she cradled the phone, with a sigh of relief, when it rang again. It was Vic calling from Vegas. After chatting a bit, enquiring about Lisa, Bella and everyone at the restaurant, she told him to hang on while she searched out Hawk who, fortunately, was working in the stables that day.

At a near run, she went to the stables only to stop short at the low, supposedly sexy sound of Brenda's voice.

"You know, Hawk, it would be fun to take a ride when you're finished here," she said, moving so that the side of her breast made contact with Hawk's arm as he brushed down the mare, Babycakes. "Just you and me. Wouldn't It?"

"Brenda…" he began, strain underlying his tone.

"I don't think so," Kate said, striding forward to wedge herself between Hawk and the girl. "Vic's on the phone, Hawk," she said, taking the brush from his hand. "I'll take over here."

He frowned with concern. "Lisa?"

"No, no," Kate shook her head. "Just a friendly call."

"Good," he said, loping from the stable as he headed for the house.

Kate began applying the brush. She imagined she could hear Brenda getting ready to explode. "I thought you were going for a ride, Brenda." Kate continued brushing. "I'm afraid you'll have to ride alone now." She shifted to level a warning look at the girl. "And in the future…if you get my drift?"

With a snort almost as loud as Babycakes could make, Brenda stormed from the stables.

A few minutes later Hawk startled Kate by silently stepping up next to her. "How can a man walk so damned quietly in those heeled boots?" she demanded.

He grinned. "Practice." He lowered his voice. "Is the temptress in training gone?"

Kate nodded, sighing. "She wants your body."

He tossed his head, exactly as his stallion did. "Who doesn't?"

She rolled her eyes, and changed the subject. "Did Vic want anything in particular?"

"No," he shook his head and gave her a wry look. "He said you sounded okay and told me flat out I'd better make sure you remained okay."

"Or what?" Kate had to laugh. "Vic's in Vegas and we're here. What was he intending to do about it?"

"He said he'd have to come rescue you from me."

"Right," she drawled. "I can just see Vic, running off to the mountains to rescue me, leaving his precious, pregnant Lisa at home alone." Shaking her head as if in despair of the silly men, Kate went back to the house.

Fortunately, they didn't see hid nor hair of Brenda for several weeks. Kate was settling nicely into a routine, inside and outside of the house. She was beginning to feel if she belonged there, in the mountains, in the house, with Hawk.

Dangerous feeling, she told herself. She didn't belong there. She was there simply because of a good and kind man…who didn't even believe in romantic love.

Kate had learned of his attitude one evening while he was watching a game and she was reading a book, a historical romance novel. During half-time, after fetching glasses of wine for them both, he asked her what she was reading. Not thinking anything of his curiosity, she told him, adding a brief resume of the story. To her surprise, he raised a skeptical brow.

"What?" she asked.

"That stuff—fantasy, love till the end of time. You don't really believe in that, do you?"

If she hadn't, she was beginning to, Kate thought. Aloud she merely answered in a teasing tone, "Could happen."

"Uh-huh." Without another word, he turned his attention to the second half of the game.

"You don't believe in love?" Kate said, snagging his attention away from the TV. "What about Vic and Lisa and Ted and Carol? They appear very much in love."

"Okay, yes, I know they are in love, but they have their problems, too. It's certainly not the fairy-tale, happily-ever-after stuff."

He shrugged. "Personally, I've never experienced the feeling."

Kate fought against the crushed sensation his words caused inside her. She wanted to cry out against the ache in her chest, the sense of loss and deflation. But she didn't cry out, instead lifted her head and simply said, "Too bad." Picking up her book, she walked away. "I'm going to bed."

The days sped by. They had a light snowfall in early November. The snow didn't last. They gathered at Ted and Carol's house for Thanksgiving. Hawk provided the huge turkey he had in his freezer chest.

As the season turned from chilly fall to cold winter, Kate worked with the horses until Hawk taught her how to keep the records of the ranch and the bloodlines of the horses on his computer.

Two weeks before Christmas, Hawk drove Kate into Durango. He went shopping for groceries and ranch supplies, leaving her to do her Christmas shopping. First she bought gifts for her father, stepmother and the children, and Vic, Lisa and Bella, and had them packaged and sent to Virginia and Las Vegas. Then she shopped for what she thought would be thoughtful but not personal gifts for Hawk.

As a rule, Christmas shopping had always been fun for Kate, but not this year. She simply couldn't get into the holiday mood. By next year she'd be gone—who knew where. She wasn't even sure she had done the right thing buying gifts for Hawk. She didn't even know if he celebrated Christmas.

Glancing at her watch, Kate saw that it was almost time to meet Hawk at the truck. Well, she thought, shrugging, what's done is done. She could always take back the gifts if he didn't want them. The very idea made her sad.

Kate felt a lot better about the whole holiday thing the next week when Hawk dragged a large pine tree onto the porch to dry.

When he set it up in the living room a couple days later, Kate got even more into the spirit of the holiday. If there was only to be one Christmas with Hawk, Kate was determined to make the best of it.

Christmas morning, both Kate and Hawk slept in late. Well, they weren't asleep all morning. Tossing back the down comforter, they worked up a pleasant sweat exchanging certain Christmas gifts.

Later, freshly showered and dressed, they

breakfasted on coffee and Christmas cookies as they sat together on the floor to exchange material Christmas presents.

There were small items with Hawk's name on the tags: new tough leather work gloves, a braided belt and a handheld computer game. He was very obviously surprised and pleased with the handmade cable-knit sweater in the Black Watch colors, imported from Scotland, that Kate had ordered for him online.

There and then, he pulled off the sweatshirt he had minutes before put on, replacing it with the sweater she had chosen for him.

After he had finished opening his gifts, Hawk slid a small pile of presents toward Kate.

As excited as a kid, Kate dove into the pile. Carefully unwrapping each gift, she revealed a delicate handwrought sterling silver bracelet, which she immediately insisted Hawk fasten on her wrist. The next package contained an Amazon.com gift certificate for a hefty amount, which she exclaimed over. The last package held the cashmere scarf Hawk had bought in Vegas, supposedly for his sister. The scarf earned Hawk what he declared to be a teeth-rattling kiss.

One morning a few days later, Kate had been out helping in the stables, and noticing it was time to start lunch, she headed for the house. Upon entering, she noticed at once that the door to Hawk's bedroom was open. Kate clearly recalled shutting the door before leaving the house.

Walking quietly down the hallway, she stepped inside the room, to find Brenda rifling through Hawk's dresser drawers, touching his clothes.

"What are you doing in here, Brenda?" Kate's voice was soft but icy.

"I…I…" The girl stopped trying to answer and glared at Kate. "He belongs to me, you know."

"Really?" Kate smiled.

Brenda flinched at Kate's cold expression, then lashed out in anger. "Yes, he does. He is mine. Who are you but a Vegas tramp who thought she had bagged a rich rancher?" She was breathing heavily. "Well, I'm telling you, bitch, when he's tired of his new playmate, he'll toss you out and I'll have him back."

"You've got a lot to learn, young lady," Kate said, holding on to her temper. "Hawk is my husband. Other than being the daughter of his friend, you mean nothing to him."

"That's a lie," Brenda shouted. "I'll be around long after you've been tossed out."

"Oh, Brenda," Kate sighed. "I think what you need is a swift kick in the ass to jar some sense into you."

"And I've got the boot to do it," Hawk said from the doorway. "Go home, Brenda, and don't come back until you've learned how to act your age."

"Damn you both," Brenda cried out like a spoiled kid, tears running down her face, sniffing, as she ran out of the room. They heard the front door slam.

Drawing a deep breath of relief, Hawk smiled at Kate. "Thanks, Kate. I do believe the message finally got through to her. I appreciate it."

"Anytime, cowboy," she said. "Now, what do you want for dinner?"

He laughed. She joined in with him.

The next day Jack drove Brenda to the airport to put her on a plane. She was going back to her mother's home.

Winter brought with it heavy snow. On the morning of the heaviest snowfall, Hawk confined Kate to the house. He didn't advise her to stay inside, he issued a flat order. The name Jeff immediately sprang into her mind.

"Hawk," the sharp edge of her voice stopped him in his tracks as he headed for the back door.

"Yes?" He turned frowning.

"I'm an adult, a full-grown woman. I will not be ordered around, not by you or any other man." Placing her hands on her hips, she stared defiantly at him.

Hawk's drawn eyebrows rose. "Kate, I'm

only insisting you stay inside because I know how treacherous the terrain can become outside in this weather. It's for your own safety."

Kate lifted a hand to flick a shooing motion at him. "You go to work, and leave me to worry about my safety." Without waiting for any argument from him, she stormed down the hallway and into their room to make the bed. She fully expected him to follow her. Her shoulders slumped and she felt like crying when he didn't.

Damn, she didn't know what she wanted anymore. Now there was a rift between her and Hawk, but Kate knew she had to carry on. A deal was a deal. Only their deal was now a mostly silent one. They spoke only when necessary. The quiet wore on Kate's nerves. Tired of it, she went outside to stomp around in the pristine snow, slamming the door behind her.

Hawk was there waiting for her when the cold finally sent her back into the house, wet and shivering.

"Feel better?" He looked tired. He sounded tired.

Kate felt ashamed for acting out like a spoiled kid. "I'm sorry, Hawk, but I will not be penned up in the house, snow or no snow."

"I can understand that," he said, his tone inflectionless. "I don't like it myself. But when I'm working some distance from the house, will you agree to confine yourself to the path the men and I made from the back of the house to the stables? I'm sure Babycakes would appreciate your company."

Kate knew that once Hawk had given her the mare to use while she was on the ranch, he had not taken Babycakes out with him to work.

"Yes, I'll agree to that."

"Thank you." He started to turn away. "I'm going to get a shower before dinner." He glanced back at her. "That is, if we're having dinner."

The shame making her uncomfortable turned to a flash of anger that zipped through her. "Of course we're having dinner," she said heatedly. "Haven't I prepared dinner every evening since I've been here?"

"Yes, Kate, you have." He gave her a half smile. "Thing is, I've gotten used to coming into the house to be greeted by the delicious aroma of whatever you're cooking. I don't smell a thing today."

Pleased by his appreciation of her cooking efforts, Kate smiled back at him while shaking her head in exasperation. "I made dinner earlier…so I could go romp in the snow. The meal is in the fridge; all it needs is warming up. It will be ready by the time you've finished your shower."

"Oh…okay." His smile now rueful, he retreated to the bedroom.

From that day forward there was a change in Hawk, in the atmosphere whenever they were together. Though he was unfailingly polite, there was very little laughter or teasing, and what smiles did touch his lips were strained.

Kate couldn't help but notice the only time he touched her during the day was obviously accidental. The nights were different, too. His lovemaking steadily grew a bit rough with an almost desperate intensity, driving Kate to heights of breathtaking pleasure she had never experienced, never dreamed could be experienced. Yet when she finally came down from the shattering high she felt empty and alone.

Longing for the easy companionship they had shared before, Kate racked her mind for a reasonable explanation for the change in him. Thinking a breath of fresh air might clear her mind, she took some sugar cubes and an apple then went to the mudroom at the back of the house and pulled on her boots and heavy jacket.

Leaving the house, Kate made her way along the path that was now almost bare due to the sudden shift to milder weather a couple of days ago. Entering the stables, she went straight to Babycakes' stall. The mare was obviously happy to see her as she nudged Kate's shoulder before lowering her head to snuffle at her jacket pocket.

"You know me too well, Miss Babycakes."
Laughing, Kate drew two sugar cubes from
her pocket and gave them to the eager horse.
When the animal was finished with the treat
she looked up, her big brown eyes staring
right into Kate's as if sensing her unhappiness
and silently asking why.

Kate's eyes and nose began to sting an
instant before she burst into tears. Once again
the mare nudged her shoulder. With no one
else to talk to, Kate poured her heart out to
her temporary pet.

"Oh, Baby, I don't know what to do."
Raising her arms, Kate cradled the mare's
large head atop her shoulder. "There's no one
else for me to talk to. I don't know Carol well
enough and I can't call Lisa, she'd get upset
and that's the last thing she needs at this stage
of her pregnancy. I won't call my father

because I've let him believe I'm so happy and so very much in love."

Kate sniffed and, moving back, she dug in her other jacket pocket for a tissue. She blew her nose. Before she was through, Babycakes nudged her again, as though telling her to go on with her tale of woe.

Smiling, crying, she stroked the long nose, swallowed and allowed the misery to spill out. "There's been a distance between us for weeks now and I hate it." The tears flowed freely. "He told me he didn't believe in love." A sob caught in her throat. "And he told me long ago he enjoyed being alone." The horse whinnied as if in commiseration. "I'm afraid he's beginning to think of me as an intrusion into his life." For a moment Kate closed her eyes, swiping her hand over her wet cheeks.

"I'm a fool, Baby," she murmured. The mare

shook her head, eliciting a weepy laugh from Kate. "Yes I am, a foolish idiot. I suggested the bargain as the perfect answer to my problem and now I have a bigger problem, a much bigger problem. I am so deep in love with Hawk I can't bear this coolness between us."

With a final sniff and a final stroke of the mare's long nose, she took the apple from her pocket and fed it to the horse. "Spring's almost here, Baby. I want winter back. I want the Hawk I knew in Vegas back." The mare finished chomping the apple and Kate turned away.

"I want, I want," she muttered, sighing as she left the stable. "And I'm talking to a horse. Sheer idiocy."

While Kate grew more quiet, more with-drawn, Hawk was wrestling with uncertainties of his own. Throughout the past few weeks the coolness in the house had nothing to do with the heating system, and everything to do with the chill between him and Kate.

Riding in late one warm afternoon in the beginning of April, Hawk walked his horse to cool him down. After grooming the roan, he stabled him then walked down the aisle of stalls to the one holding Babycakes, the mare he had given to Kate for her exclusive use while she was at the ranch. Now he couldn't think of the animal as anything other than Kate's.

Stepping into the stall of the gentle chestnut, Hawk took up a brush and began to groom her. Also, without thinking, he began softly talking to her.

"I'm in deep crap, Baby," he murmured, using Kate's nickname for the horse. "And I'm afraid you're going to be mad as hell at me." The horse nickered. "You may not believe it now," he said, as if he had heard a "no way" in the horse's noise, "but you'll understand when your mistress is gone."

The mare shook her big head. Damn, Hawk thought, for all he knew, maybe the horse did understand. Mocking himself for the very idea, he nevertheless continued talking.

"It's my fault she is going," he went on. "I deliberately built a wall of virtual silence between us." The horse snorted. "Yeah, I know, pretty stupid. But, much as I hate to admit it, even to you, I was getting scared. It started after we had a silly argument about her staying inside during the worst weather. As gentle as Kate is with you, Baby, you wouldn't believe how she blew a gasket at me for daring to give her orders."

For a moment Hawk smiled in memory of

how magnificent Kate had looked in her defiance of him. Another memory flashed and he sighed.

"But it was the night I laughed at the book she was reading, calling it a fantasy of happy-ever-after and telling her I didn't believe in that kind of thing. She walked away from me, and since then has stayed away from me, there but cool and distant. I could kick myself in the ass. When she walked away a knot settled in my gut. It's been getting tighter and tighter with each passing day."

By pure coincidence, Hawk felt sure, the mare moved her large head, trapping Hawk's head against her long neck. The curry brush fell unnoticed to the ground. Hawk rested his forehead on her smooth coat.

"And now our bargain time is up, Baby. Kate's going to leave us both." A shudder ran through him. The horse shook her head. "I know, you don't want her to go. You think she's yours. Well, I don't want her to go, either. I love her. I—who has never felt anything deep or lasting for any woman—love Kate more than my own life."

Hawk shuddered again and felt a sudden sting in his eyes. Tears rolled down his face. Damn, he never cried, hadn't shed a tear since he was nine or ten. He didn't make a sound but the tears continued to flow until the mare moved her head and he noticed the wet spot on her coat.

"Sorry, girl," he drew a deep breath, scrubbed his big hands over his face and stood up straight. "I don't suppose you have any suggestions? No? I didn't think so." Stepping back out of the stall, he closed the gate. The mare stuck her head out and with a shaky laugh Hawk stroked her face. Her big brown eyes appeared sad.

"I'll see what I can do for the two of us, sweetheart," he promised. "I'll beg her to stay if I have to."

Stepping out onto the porch for a breather late one afternoon early in April, Kate felt the first mild breeze of spring. The last remnants of happiness and contentment she had enjoyed until recently with Hawk, while working, laughing, making love with him, dissolved like the small patches of snow from the last snowfall.

It was almost time for her to leave. Her six months were up. Sadness welled up in her; tears stung her eyes. Where had the days gone, one after another, fading from month to month? Kate loved spring, but she wanted winter back. She didn't want to return to Vegas or to her father's farm. She didn't want to go, couldn't bear the thought of being away from Hawk forever.

But his coolness, his near silence for nearly two months, said it all to Kate. It was time for her to go, to give Hawk's life back to him.

Tears streaming down her face, Kate squared her shoulders and walked into the house. A deal was a deal. Pain twisted in her chest as she remembered the way they had "double" sealed their deal with a handshake and two kisses.

Going to Hawk's bedroom, *their* bedroom, Kate swiped the tears from her cheeks, impatient with herself for wanting, longing to renege on their bargain.

It wasn't fully six months yet; she could wait until the end of the month. The thought wriggled its way into her head, tempting her to hang on to him every last minute.

Kate shook away the thought. It would only get harder for both of them if she lingered longer. Dragging her suitcases from the closet, she began packing her things. For a moment, she stroked the beautiful scarf Hawk had given to her at Christmas. The tears started again.

Ignoring them, sniffing, Kate continued until she had packed all her belongings but the clothes she was wearing and the those she planned to wear tomorrow, when Hawk, she hoped, would take the time to drive her to the airport.

Hawk entered the house and frowned at the lack of aromatic cooking scents wafting on the air. It was quiet, too quiet. There was no sight or sound of Kate.

He smiled softly, thinking she had probably lain across the bed to take a nap and had overslept. His smile growing sad, he went down the hallway to their bedroom, planning to take advantage of the opportunity to join her on the bed…and sleep had nothing to do with his plan.

The door was partially open. Quietly pushing it in, he stepped inside the bedroom and stopped dead. Kate was sitting on the side of the bed, her suitcases on the floor next to her, unchecked tears running down her flushed face.

"Kate?" Hawk crossed to her in three long strides. "What's wrong? Why are you crying? And what are your suitcases doing here on the floor?"

She drew a long, shuddering breath and, without looking up at him, said, "I'm leaving, Hawk. The six months are almost up. Will you drive me to the airport tomorrow, please?"

"No." His heart was racing.

Her head flew up and she stared at him. "Oh, well, if you're too busy, perhaps Jack or Ted can take me."

"No." Now he could hardly breathe.

"Why?" She swiped a hand over her red-rimmed eyes.

Hawk couldn't stand seeing her cry. Kicking her luggage aside, he grasped her by the shoulders and pulled her up to face him.

"I don't want you to go, Kate." He heard the pained rawness in his voice and didn't care. "I want you to stay here with me."

"After the coolness between us for two months, you want to extend my stay?" The tears had stopped but her lips still trembled.

"No, dammit!" Throwing caution and possibly his hope of continued happiness away, he gazed directly into her red, puffy eyes and said, "Will you marry me, Kate?"

She blinked, then blinked again. "Hawk, what are you saying? We *are* married."

He shook his head. "I mean, will you stay married to me? Can we renew our vows to each other, for real this time?" He caught his breath. "Kate, I love you so much. If you leave me now, I'll live. But I won't like it."

Kate had the audacity to laugh…right before she threw herself against him, wrapped her arms round his neck and joyously shouted, "Yes, yes, yes, I'll stay, Hawk, because maybe you'll live if I go…but I don't know if I will. I love you." She raised her voice even louder. "I love you, Hawk McKenna. I believe I have from our first kiss."

* * * * *

R